Daddy's Girl

*To my Father*

Linda Allin

# Daddy's Girl

© 2005 Linda Allin
Herstellung und Verlag: Books on Demand GmbH, Norderstedt
ISBN 3-8334-2106-1

# Chapter One

## June 1996

### Valerie

I reach up behind the iron bedstead, switch on the light and tell my father to die.

"Walk towards the light, Dad," I say, just as my brother told me to.

"I don't need to be there," he said. My New Age, psychic sibling.

I do. I cradle my father's head in one hand, slip the elastic band over storkwhite hair and put the oxygen mask on his bedside table between grapes and clusters of printed prayer cards which multiply every night. Each morning there are more. Is there a bat vicar in the rafters, resting by day and flying out at dusk to claim a soul or two?

The plastic mouthpiece of the mask is lukewarm. The beak of a dying bird. The heavy black cylinder of gas by the side of the bed pumps on, oblivious. I lay his head on the pillow. Gently does it. I don't want to hurt him. Not anymore. The doctor says it makes no difference. His brain's gone. Nothing left for him to feel with. Paul, my brother, says that's crap. I choose to believe him. Bugger medicine, I think, wrapping the hand that's outside the blankets in mine. Doctors don't know everything. Dad's fingers are like curled claws, the nails scratch at my palm. Longer than he'd ever let them grow. Poofter's nails, he'd call them if the stroke hadn't cut his communication cord for good.

For a few seconds he breathes on, great gulping breaths. Then whoosh, a long sigh leaves angel bubbles dancing at the corners of his mouth. I wipe them away. I don't want him to die messy.

He'd hate that. I wait, holding my breath in case he starts again. It wouldn't be the first time he'd stopped then revved up again as if to say, "Gotcha!" I stare at his chest but it doesn't move. The navy blue M and S easy-care polyester is still.

"Thank God," Mum sighs.

I bend down and kiss the transparent skin of his cheek.

Mum peels my fingers from his hand. One by one.

"Let him go, love."

I watch her bend down and kiss him, realising I've never seen that before. They didn't kiss in public. My father wasn't a toucher. She whispers in his ear and strokes his forehead, something he'd never let her do if he were alive. "Get off, Stella," he'd snap. "Stop messing me about."

I wonder if they ever kissed at all.

I draw back the curtain – nursery blue dotted with yellow, mop-head chrysanths – and call the nurse. My voice booms through the silent ward. Got it from him, that teacher's voice that can stop a third-form punch-up at fifty paces. Every bed's taken but you'd never guess, the other patients lie so still. Not a sigh, a sneeze, not even the rustle of a sheet to give them away. I hear the thud-slide-thump of Jasmine's Scholl sandals long before she sails into view, swaying from side to side, ebony beads glistening on her forehead like darkened portholes, smile beaming out with the force of the QE2's lights across murky Atlantic waters.

"He fought it," Mum whispers, "to the very end."

That and everything else around him.

"Shall we wait?" I ask Jasmine. Looking up her huge prow – six-foot five if she's an inch – I feel dwarfed but not threatened.

"Didn't half frighten me," he said, "the first time I saw her."

I'd never thought of him as being afraid. Other fathers maybe. My Dad? Never.

Jasmine shakes her head. "No. You needn't upset yourselves. Doctor's on his way."

"What happens now?"

I realise it's a stupid question as soon as I've asked but I really don't know. Dad's the first corpse I've ever clapped eyes on.

Jasmine fiddles with the diamond splinter on her engagement finger and gives us a warm, confiding smile.

"Well," she says, "I'll give him a good wash and put a clean night-shirt on. Tidy him up."

I don't want the three-volume novel, the Reader's Digest would do just fine, but now Jasmine's warmed to her subject, she's not going to let anyone interrupt her.

"Then I'll lay him out, give his hair a good brush. He had lovely hair, didn't he? Sort of Omo white, or Ariel." She chuckles. "Adverts on the brain, me. Anyway, I'll make him look all nice, so you can say your goodbyes."

"We already have," Mum says.

"Oh. Well." Jasmine sighs as if disappointed we won't be there to admire her handiwork. "Then the doctor'll certify death and a porter'll come and get him."

Her voice is a smooth, rolling lilt, her tone matter-of-fact. Death's no stranger here. He's the most frequent visitor on a geriatric ward.

"Might as well go home, then," Mum says.

"Yes," Jasmine agrees. "Come back for the death certificate to-morrow. I'll have his things ready."

She sounds relieved to get shot of us, which is no surprise. She's alone on the ward tonight. The inmates are ovaltined, talcumed, tucked in as tight as King Tut, but it's the lull before the storm. Soon yells, nightmare screams and thuds of bodies that have wormed their way out of blanket embalming will start and keep her rolling from one six-pack room to the next. One carer, twenty-four patients. A normal night on a National Health ward.

Our shoes squeak on the grey lino as we creep out. None of the patients say goodbye. Not Arthur or Grandad, not even Ronald, the plum pudding on legs who found his sprig of mistletoe on a geriatric ward when he shouldn't even have been there. They're stiff in their beds, rigor-mortissed with terror it's their turn next. You can almost see the prayers wafting up through the eau-de-nil emulsioned ceiling. Not me, dear Lord, please. Take him in the next bed. The ward door swings shut behind us, we link hands and walk down the corridor, slow marching towards the Exit sign. Walking towards the light.

## September 1995

### Jack

I was having a good clear-out today, sorting the bottom cupboard in the front room unit. I've got to get it done while Stella's away. She's a right hoarder, won't let you chuck a thing. I came across these old photos of Valerie. Some of me holding her. About ten days old, she was. That's how long they kept you in hospital. I don't know how long it is now, not having any grandchildren, but in the fifties women were in for a week at least, to give them a proper rest.

"I *am* going in to see them," I insisted, pushing past Matron. She was the build of Oliver Hardy, just not quite as attractive. She grabbed me by the sleeve but I shook her off sharpish and marched along the corridor clutching my five quids' worth of chrysanths. Didn't have a clue where I was going. I reckoned I'd find Stella and the baby eventually if I just kept walking. It wasn't a big place. One of those posh houses on Bishop's Avenue – Millionaire's Row, they called it – bought by the council as an annexe of the North Middlesex Hospital. I was chuffed Stella was there, not down with the hoi polloi in Fore Street.

"Stop right this minute, Mr Sterling," Matron barked. "This has gone far enough." She was clutching at my sleeve, striding along beside me like a sergeant major, head held back, eyes and mouth three thin lines. A face from the past flashed through my mind, made me want to knock her block off but I carried on walking, didn't even tell her to get her clammy mitts off my best suit. My only suit, as it happened.

Then luck ran out on me. I took a corner too sharp and me and Matron collided with two porters pushing an empty trolley. From their side-of-beef bodies and lardy complexions they'd have looked more at home in an abattoir than a maternity clinic. Thank Christ that stretcher's empty, I thought. You wouldn't want patients seeing them on the way to the delivery room.

"You all right, Matron?" one of them asked. His voice told me he'd got two working brain cells and he'd given one the day off.

Matron said no, she wasn't all right.

"All I want," I said very slowly, "is to see my wife and baby."

The heavies let go of the trolley and stood, snorting in unison, blocking my path. Matron lined up beside them, glaring at me as if I was something to be swilled down the sluice.

"I've told you, Mr Sterling," she said, "mother and baby are doing well. There's nothing to be concerned about."

I wasn't having any of that old toffee. "Why won't you let me see them, then?"

"Because visiting time is between six and seven pm. It is now seven-fifteen."

"But surely you can make an exception? I wasn't there at the birth..."

"I should hope not," she sniffed. "Where on earth would we be with fathers getting in Doctor's way? Fainting all over the place and being a nuisance."

"Nuisance," repeated Blockhead Number One, wrinkling a nose that was crying out for a ring through it.

I thought, one more word from you, but my arms were full of flowers and I knew it would do no good to start a fight in a clinic.

"You may come back tomorrow," Matron said, gracious now she thought she was winning. "Mother and baby need to rest. Mr Stamp and Mr Perkins here will escort you off the premises. Good evening."

Off she trundled, apron creaking with starch, stockings chafing thighs that'd snap off your hand if it got between them. There was a bit of a scuffle when the bullocks tried to get hold of me. I lost my rag, the chrysanths lost their heads. This worked in my favour, though 'cos it put the bullocks in a quandary. What was more important? Throwing me out or clearing up the mess before Matron clapped eyes on it? They stood there gawping so I nabbed the chance and shot off down the corridor. Sod the lot of you, I thought. This is my child and you won't let me see her because of your poxy rules and regulations. How dare you. How dare the bloody lot of you!

I'd have been all right if Matron hadn't been lurking round the corner, polishing the watch on her twin-cauldron bosom. "You really are wasting my time, Mr Sterling," she said. "It would make things so much easier for us all if you'd do as you're told and come back tomorrow."

"But I tried my damndest to get here earlier."

I'd taken the call in Pettifer's office and asked straight away.

"I trust your wife is well?" He looked up from a haberdashery order. Head buyer, he was, and the store's chief arselicker. Wore suits I wouldn't use as snotrags. "Will we really sell these gilt buttons? They seem extremely expensive to me."

"My wife's fine," I said. "She's had the baby. A little girl."

"Oh," he sniffed. "Well, I expect... Next time..."

"No, no, no," I said. "I'm over the moon."

"Good," he said. "If you think the buttons will sell..."

I felt like telling him to stuff his buttons. "I was wondering whether I could have the rest of the afternoon off."

It was just gone five. The store would only be open another half-hour. I'd lose a bit of commission but I didn't give a damn. I didn't need money to spend on myself.

"I'm afraid that won't be possible," he said. "If I make an exception for you, everyone will be wanting the same."

"I don't think that's likely," I said, "not with the average age of the staff." I shouldn't have said it but he'd got my goat. And anyway it was true. Stella and me were the only ones more than nodding distance away from our coffins. The rest of them looked as if they were on loan from Boris Karloff. For a split second I thought about walking out, telling him to stuff his bloody job, but I didn't. We needed the money too much for that.

"Now, Mr Sterling," Matron said. "We'll see you again tomorrow."

The heavies closed in and frogmarched me back to the entrance, grinning all the way.

"I'll be back, you bastards," I muttered. "And God help the pair of you if you're around."

I knew I'd have to get another load of flowers but I didn't care. I wanted my wife and child to have the very best. Nothing less would do.

## Valerie

"I wish he was here," Mum says, looking at the frilly white waves on the Swiss lake. The one-forty-five boat sounds its horn and steams past the balcony, tourists lining the railings, both adults and children waving furiously. They can't be waving at us so we don't wave back.

"Everyone says you look so much better for coming here on your own." I'm deadheading daisies, getting the tubs ready for winter.

Snip, snip. Off with their heads. "It does you good to get away." It would do her good to get shot of him full stop, but I can't say that now, can I?

"But he's never seen all this." She waves in queenmotherly manner, encompassing the balcony and flat. "It's like something out of a magazine."

"He could come if he wanted to."

She sighs. "He says he wouldn't know what to do with himself. He doesn't like window shopping."

I toss the daisy heads into a plastic container. Green for organic, grey for standard household refuse, black for aluminium. When it comes to rubbish, the Swiss have got life sorted. "That's just an excuse and you know it. We don't have to go shopping. We could do other things." I wrack my brain wondering what. He doesn't like the cinema, isn't a foodie, can't stand museums and gets giddy going up mountains. What else is there?

She takes a sip of tea. "He says it would be different if there was someone for him to talk to."

I mutter a few expletives and move on to the busy lizzies, ripping off every flower that has the temerity to droop. "Why can't he talk to us, for God's sake?" This is purely rhetorical. He never has and he never will.

She puts down her teacup and returns to a slice of *Kirschtorte*, which is wilting pinkly in the sun. "How much *Kirsch* is in this cake? It's making me feel quite drunk. You know what your Dad means."

"'Course I do." I take a gulp of my first afternoon spritzer. "A bloke. Every girl's essential accessory."

She tilts her plate, fills her spoon with clear, sweet booze. "He's just worried about you here all on your own."

"I've been here twenty years. What does he think's going to happen? And if he's so worried, why doesn't he phone? Wouldn't hear from him if it wasn't for you."

He wrote to me once. 1981, I think it was.

"You should know your Dad by now. Still waters."

I finish my spritzer and go back to poking plants.

It's an English balcony, this. Nothing Helvetic. No Sound of Music red geraniums, just lobelia, lavender and the prickliest of roses. It's amazing how British you become abroad, dashing to the station to get the Sunday Times, shopping at supermarkets that sell Marmite and Frank Cooper's marmalade, clinging to a Laura Ashley, Earl Grey country that only exists in the glossies. I stopped buying Cosmopolitan last month and took out a subscription to Good Housekeeping. I'll be ordering twinsets from catalogues and wearing pearls next, God help me.

"He doesn't talk to anyone except children," I say. "That says it all."

"He thinks the world of you."

I nod because I love her but I know better. The trouble with my father is that he doesn't like people. He'd rather be on his own, beak stuck in one of his stupid war novels, only coming up for air when it's time for food prepared by his faithful drudge. I don't think he knows how the cooker works.

"It's getting too hot for me," she says, "I'm going to write some postcards, make myself another cuppa. Want one?"

"No, thanks."

I stamp on a shiny black beetle just landed on the terracotta floor. "Still half a bottle of Chablis. No point wasting it."

"I love that poster," she says, nodding in at the living room. "The Magic Flute, isn't it?"

I pick up a trowel and tip the tiny fluorescent corpse into the bin. "Yep." The Queen of the Night floats dead centre in a sky of stars, far above Tamino, Pamina and Zarastro. Bought it years ago. It doesn't fit the new place but I can't bring myself to throw it out.

*

In the evening we sit at a window table in the *Hecht*, sipping wine as crisp as starched linen, poring over a menu so large we can't see each other when holding it up.

"How about Italy for your birthday?"

She frowns. "That would be lovely, dear, but I'll have to see what your Dad says. He might want to go himself. Think I'll have the perch. I love that mayonnaise. So light."

"You know he won't. How many times have you heard him say he hates the place?"

She smiles. "He might change his mind."

"That'll be the day." He tends them well, his prejudices, just as I do my roses.

"Well, he was…"

"… there in the war. So were other blokes. Things have changed since then."

Mrs Rüttiman, sombrely elegant in black silk, comes over to take our order. She suggests pike, after which the restaurant is named.

"We'll both have the perch," I say, "pike's too fiddly." Mrs Rüttimann nods and glides off to the kitchen, patent Bally pumps swishing on the deep-pile carpet.

"And if he hates to be reminded," I say, "why does he spend all his time reading those idiotic war books?"

She shrugs and looks out of the window. Couples stroll along the lakeside, some pushing prams, others with arms entwined. Teenagers lounge, legs dangling in the water, torsos swaying to the thump of ghetto blasters, while supine tourists lie on pedalos that bob up and down in the wake of the evening's Fondue Boat.

I glance at a couple on a bench by the lake. "Max reads them, too." Max Fuchs – love and bane of my life. I still like to say his name out loud.

"What?" Mum tears a brown roll in two, scattering crumbs over the tablecloth.

"War novels. Max likes them."

They're all he ever reads with his classes. One day, taking the long way to my classroom so I could walk past his, I saw a flour-faced kid rush out and vomit all over the floor. Couldn't take the blood and guts, I reckon.

Mum purses her lips. "I really don't see how you can compare your father to that pig."

"I'm not. Just saying there are certain similarities."

They're both members of the Advanced Bastards Club for one thing.

She nibbles at her roll. "Have you heard from KM?"

"No."

She smears her last bite of bread with a wedge of butter, "Now, he was one your Dad really did like. Never understood why you had to get divorced."

Mrs Rüttimann and a waiter place two glass plates on the damask table cloth. "A little *amuse-bouche*," she explains, "a *goujon* of pike on a bed of julienned leek with mustard sauce. *Bon Appetit.*"

## Jack

I've known they were there a long time. Only had the guts to look today. Thank Christ I'm on my own. Stella'd wonder what the hell I was up to, bent over with my head between my knees. "Queer old coot," she'd say. She's buggered off to Nigel's for her weekly shampoo and gossip. Hope it cheers her up. She's been like a wet week ever since she got back from Switzerland.

I'm in the bathroom, naked from the waist down, standing on tiptoe in front of the mirror. There they are, plain as dumplings on a plate. Next to my own balls, two scaled-down duplicates.

"Shit!" I say to my reflection. "Toe rags!"

I know what they are, you see. Aneurisms. Can't be anything good, sounding like that, can they? Ugly, hissing word, like air seeping out of a life jacket.

The doctor explained it all last time. The walls of your artery swell up like an inner tube. If your number's up, they burst and you're a goner. Six years ago that was, just before I retired.

Nearly copped it then. I would have if Stella'd not kept nagging me to go back to the doctor's. Old Bertha Braston was giving me Milk of Magnesia, telling me to go away and stop wasting her time.

"You've been eating too much stodgy food," she said, peering at me over her bifocals.

Stella was having none of it. "I'm making an appointment with Dr Patel," she said. "It can't be indigestion or you wouldn't have that great lump in the middle of your chest."

It stuck out, clear as a cricket ball under my vest.

He took one look, that Dr Patel, and called the ambulance. He said he'd seen one of these aneurism things at medical school and you had to act fast.

Wouldn't even let me go home, he was that worried. I had to phone Stella and tell her to pack me a bag. That ambulance raced up to town, blue light flashing and everything. Eyore! Eyore! Like something off the telly. If it hadn't been my life on the line, I'd have enjoyed every minute. I didn't have to wait like you normally do, sitting on those plastic chairs till your arse merges with the seat. They got the top man straight away. Mr Macbeth. Not plain 'doctor' but 'mister'. That made me feel better.

"We're not letting you out of our sight, Mr Sterling," he said. "We'll operate tonight and I'll give you a bodyguard while I set things up. Just to be on the safe side."

Nice little thing. Blonde with blue eyes. Reminded me of Valerie only shorter. Julia, her name was.

"I'm the junior on Mr Macbeth's team," she said. "It's the best in the country so you've got nothing to worry about."

"I'm not worried," I said, but I let her hold my hand.

Wonderful place, that Bart's. They only have the top doctors there. I wouldn't have got better treatment anywhere. Still took me a while to get back on my feet, though. It was a major piece of plumbing, not like having your toenails clipped. And now they're back. Like some rotten re-run on the telly. *Morecambe and Wise and the Aneurisms*. Run in the family, that's the trouble. The old man had them, that's what finished him off. Gordon might have got them if he'd lived long enough.

Better give them a ring. Tomorrow sometime. Bart's, of course. I'm not going to that local dump. Bloody awful place. The staff are all coons. Hardly ever see a white face. Now, at Bart's I didn't see so much as one single black. That tells you something, doesn't it? And Mr Macbeth said I could go back any time.

"Once you've been our patient," he said, "we'll always take you back."

It's like you've got an account there and you can draw on it any time you need to. Reassuring, that is. Think I've perked up a bit already.

"Hang on a minute!" I shout, scooting downstairs. I can see who it is through the porch door – the tyke from the florist's round the corner. Looks like he could do with a dose of Baby Bio himself, scruffy little runt. He sells good stuff, though, I'll say that for him. He's holding a big bouquet, must have cost a fortune.

"Mrs Sterling?"

"Should know by now," I say. "You've delivered enough to this address. From Switzerland, I'll bet."

I put them on the draining board and get Stella's two big vases. The tyke's done a good job – roses, those fancy daisy things and chrysanths. I read somewhere they're funeral flowers in France. Stella's always loved them, though. I dump the roses in one vase – keep all the thorny buggers together – and put the daisies and chrysanths in the other. All colours the chrysanths are, just like the ones I took to the nursing home when Valerie was born. When I finally managed to see her, she was twenty-four hours old and I was livid. No father would stand for it nowadays but that's the way things were then. Men weren't supposed to be interested in babies and a lot of men I knew were grateful.

On the way to the hospital I'd stopped off at the florist's again. I was planning to take roses – as many as I could get for what was left of my paltry wages. Sod food and bus fares, I'd decided. The walk to work would do me good and I'd sweet-talk the girls in the canteen for grub. The first thing I saw were rows of green buckets covering the floor. They were full of chrysanths, all the colours from gold to purple, big bushy heads on them. They looked like oversized powder puffs, rich and velvety, smacking of wealth and luxury. All the things I wanted my wife and kid to have.

I started off with the gold. "I'll have half a dozen of those." Then the same of the bronze. There were some very posh-looking red things in the bucket next door so I said I'd have some of them, too. Suddenly I couldn't stop. I had to have six from every bucket in the shop. It seemed mean to leave a colour out. That left two or three flowers in each of the buckets, which looked daft.

"You won't sell those," I said to the girl. "Might as well give me them, too."

"I'll split them up, shall I?" she said. "You can take some and I'll deliver the rest in the van."

"Make a few bunches and put a bit of paper round them. That'll be fine."

They weren't heavy, just a bit awkward. The petals kept tickling my chin. I caused quite a stir walking down Palmer's Green High Street. And when I got on the bus, the conductress wouldn't take the fare. Gave me a cracker of a smile and said she hoped her husband would do the same for her.

There was a right commotion at the clinic, nurses racing round looking for vases, pots, anything to put the flowers in. Had to use fire-buckets in the end. Stella said she'd only been able to see my legs and feet when I walked in. She'd known it was me, though. No-one else's husband would do anything so mad.

Matron had to put her spoke in, of course. She said the flowers'd have to go in the corridor overnight. They'd take the oxygen and that wouldn't be good for the mothers. Nurses didn't mind, though. They said they'd be happy to cart them in and out. I made a mental note to take them a pair of nylons each for their trouble.

When Stella put the baby in my arms, I nearly blubbed right there in front of them all. I felt as if I'd been given the world wrapped in a white woolly shawl. I took Valerie over to the window and showed her the avenue outside the clinic.

"This is what you're going to have," I said.

I told her how much her mother and I had wanted her, how we were going to do everything for her.

I was standing there chatting away to her, the pair of us happy as sand boys, when the staff nurse came over.

"Baby's had enough now, Mr Sterling," she said, reaching up to take her out of my arms. "We mustn't tire her out."

I'm not giving her back yet, I thought. I've only just got hold of her. I gave the nurse my best smile, the one I use on Rosy in the canteen when I'm after an extra helping of chips. "Just a few more minutes."

It worked. It always does.

She must have taken me literally, daft girl, 'cos she was back in two shakes of a monkey's tail.

"Let's be having you, Mr Sterling," she smiled, "All the other fathers have gone."

As she stepped towards me, I took a step back. I didn't do it on purpose. We were like a couple who'd been dancing together for years. One steps forward, the other automatically goes into reverse. She did it again, so I did, too. And before you could say Jack Robinson, we were waltzing round the room. Every time she got near enough to make a lunge for the baby, I'd twirl out of her way. If it'd been down to me, we'd have gone on like that all night but Stella called out, "Be careful, Jack. You'll make the baby dizzy," and Valerie woke up.

She didn't cry, she just stared up at me. They say babies can't focus when they're small, they haven't got a clue who you are. Bollocks. My kid knew damn well who she was looking at.

I gave her a kiss and handed her back to the nurse. "See you tomorrow."

"Yes, Mr Sterling," she said. "We'll look forward to it."

Didn't have the heart to tell the silly thing I wasn't talking to her. I had a word with Stella then buggered off. Had to leg it all the way back to Palmer's Green but I didn't care. I was walking on air all the way.

# Chapter Two

## October 1995

### Jack

"I know you," says a smooth Scottish drawl, rich and oaky as finest single malt. He's wearing a pinstripe, some Mayfair tailor's, I'll bet. Pink shirt, gold cufflinks, navy silk tie. A Turnbull and Asser man if ever I saw one. He's impressive, my surgeon. And it's not just the clothes. He's the kind of bloke your eyes are drawn to. You don't notice anyone else in the room.

I smile and tell him I've been in before and he did the operation.

"Yes, of course," he says, like the manager of the Ritz recognising a guest he hasn't seen for a while. "Mr Sterling. Aneurism of the aorta, wasn't it? Come back for a refit?"

He shoos Stella away and examines my lumps as gently as if they were the Crown Jewels. Warms his hands first. A real gent. His fingers are long and slim, artistic-looking. You'd think he was a pianist if you didn't know.

I dreamt about him once, just after my operation. He was standing on the banks of the Dee, salmon fishing. They were leaping out of the water at him, each fish bigger than the last, as if they felt honoured to be caught by such a great man. Funny the tricks your mind plays when you're sick.

I hoist up my bags and he calls Stella back. "Well," he says, "you're a wee bit older than you were the first time and I won't insult your intelligence by saying it isn't a major undertaking. You'll be spending a fair few days with us if you decide to go ahead."

"What are my chances?"

"I'm perfectly confident I can give you another ten years," he says, eyes lighting up like Loch Ness on a sunny day.

My heart leaps. I'm not afraid, not a bit. In a strange sort of way I'm starting to feel bloody marvellous.

"What if he doesn't have the operation?" Stella pipes up.

Trust her to put a spoke in.

"Whheeell," Mr Macbeth says, "the aneurisms will probably burst."

"When?" she asks.

She's got no respect sometimes. Who does she think she's talking to?

"Oh, shut up," I say. "Whose body is it?"

"It's a perfectly justified question, Mr Sterling," my surgeon says. Obviously used to dealing with difficult women. "Your wife's right to be concerned. We can't really say, Mrs Sterling."

"So he might live for years with them?"

"Yes."

I can tell what she's thinking and I'm not having any of it. "I want that operation," I say, looking straight at Mr Macbeth.

"Why don't you go away and think about it?" he says.

"You're six years older than last time, Jack," Stella nags. "And you've lost so much weight lately."

"Don't talk such tommyrot. I weigh what I've always weighed. And I don't need to think about it." I look at Mr Macbeth, assurance oozing out of him like syrup from a treacle duff. "If you say you can give me another ten years, I believe you."

"Then you're more of a fool than I thought," Stella mutters.

We don't talk on the way home. I don't understand her. Why the hell can't she be happy for me? Ten more years. It's a gift, a new bloody life.

\*

"Why don't you stay in the other room?" she says, switching on the light. It's been getting dark early since we put the clocks back. "Finish your tea and watch the end of *Lawrence of Arabia*."

She doesn't want me in the kitchen, if the truth were known. Says I get under her feet. Bloody cheek. I drag a stool in front of the fridge. "My tea's gone cold and I've never liked that film. Too much sand."

Stella snorts but it's true. So much sand you start picking it out from between your teeth. "If you're going to get in my way, you might as well do something useful. Pass me the suet, would you? It's just inside the door, on the shelf with the butter."

I hand her the suet, take the butter out of the fridge, straighten the wrapper then put it back on the right shelf. "What do you want suet for?"

"To make a camel coat. What do you think? I'm doing some dumplings."

I hear a key in the door and think, thank Christ! Paul'll cheer his mother up. She's been right stroppy ever since the hospital. He's a handsome lad, my son. Six-foot four, nice slim build and a lovely head of hair, when he doesn't have it shorn off like something out of Belsen. Takes after my side of the family. Doesn't look a bit like his mother although she swears blind he's got her colouring. He unlaces boots heavier than the ones I wore in Italy, drops them on the mat by the back door then walks over and gives Stella a big hug and kiss – on the mouth, never on the cheek. Then he hugs me.

"All right, Dad?"

Stella rolls a dumpling into shape and drops it in the saucepan. "He's having one of his ratty days. I can't do a thing right."

"Take no notice of your mother," I say. "She's having one of her turns."

Paul takes off his tatty brown jumper. The yellow t-shirt underneath is faded and moth-eaten. You wouldn't think he had two pennies to rub together. "Hot in here," he says. "Want a fag, Dad?"

"Go on, then," I say.

"If you're going to smoke," Stella says, "you'd better open a window. But the draught won't do your father any good. And that muck won't help his lungs, either."

There was no such talk when I started. They doled out fags in the War like there was no tomorrow.

Paul reaches past Stella and opens the top window.

I inhale, hold the nicotine in my lungs as long as I can. "How's work?"

"Crap. Thinking of chucking it. What's for tea?"

"Stew." Stella whips the lid off the saucepan and a whoosh of steam mists up her glasses, which sets us off laughing.

"You'll be laughing on the other side of your face," she says to Paul, "when you've got no money."

"There are loads of jobs around, Mum. Just look in the papers."

"Not for people like you." She takes the salt and pepper out of the cupboard and bangs them down on the Formica fridge top, the usual signal the table needs setting. "You haven't got your sister's qualifications."

In a minute she'll start on about his tattoos. I don't like the bloody things, either – snakes, lizards, all sorts of muck from his wrists to his armpits, but she'll do no good going on about them.

"I don't want to spend the rest of my days loading lorries," he says. "I hate every minute of it."

"A lot of people aren't keen on their jobs," she snaps. "Your father never much liked any of his but he stuck at them, didn't you, Jack?"

"Hated most of them, as well you know."

"Leave that, Dad," Paul says, when he sees me open the cutlery drawer. "I'll do it in a minute. Look Mum, I'm not wasting my life doing something I loathe eight hours a day. Dad understands, don't you, Dad?"

"'Course I do, son." I look at the knives and forks. "Think I'll take these in."

I know it gets Stella's goat when I don't boss the kids about like she does. She says I'm copping out. I won't have it, though, she can nag as long as she likes. I've learnt my lesson the hard way. A long time ago I told someone what to do and it's haunted me every day of my life ever since.

Stella picks up a spoon and gives the stew a good stir, digging right down to the bottom, making it swirl round the pot, the dumplings bobbing on top. "Have you told your son how you got on at hospital?"

"There's nothing to tell. I got on fine." I take a tea-towel from the hook under the boiler and buff up the knives and forks. "Spurs did all right, then."

"Yeah," Paul says, "good team."

"'Course," I grin, "they haven't got Arsenal's class. Never will have."

"Arsenal are rubbish and you know it. No defence for one thing."

I put the tea-towel back on its hook, rattle the knives and forks a bit. "Beat Leeds and Villa fair and square, though. Can't argue with that."

Paul laughs. "Yeah, and lost to Chelsea."

And off we go, jawing about managers, forwards and goalies like we do every weekend. Stella calls out not to forget the serviettes. Don't know why she makes such a fuss. We never use the damn things anyway.

"How do you really feel about your op, then?" Paul says, when we're out of Stella's earshot.

"All right, son. Very confident."

He stands there at the table, looking at me, waiting.

"I am," I say. "I'm not putting it on."

I take the mats from the sideboard and set them on the cloth. Paul puts knives and forks either side, smiles when I straighten them.

"Mum's worried about you, you know."

"I don't know what for." She's had no medical training, even if she did work in a chemist's years ago. "I want that operation. I want it more than anything in the world and I'm bloody well going to have it."

Paul drifts back out to the kitchen and I follow.

He puts his arm round Stella, peers over her shoulder. "What's in the stew?"

"Chicken," she says. "Big bits, though, that I can fish out for your Dad and me. There's plenty of veg and dumplings for you, love."

Paul frowns.

Here we go, I think to myself.

"Did you use normal suet for the dumplings?"

Stella wipes her hand across her forehead. "Yes."

Paul sighs. "And what's suet made of?"

"Fat, I suppose. I don't know."

"Beef fat."

"You know he's a vegetarian," I say.

"I know he doesn't eat meat but I didn't realise he went that far."

"It's not going far, Mum," he says, lighting another cigarette.

"Well, it is to me," Stella says. "And if you're so health conscious, why do you still smoke?"

"No vegetarians eat suet, Mum."

"How on earth am I supposed to know?" She gives me a filthy look. Don't know what the hell for. I haven't done anything.

"Couldn't you fish the dumplings out?" she suggests. "There's a French stick in the freezer. Just have bread and vegetables. It's not much of a dinner, but then I'm not the fussy one."

"No," he says, looking a bit narked himself. "I'd rather not."

"Well, you can't sit at the table starving hungry, watching your father and me."

"I won't sit there watching you. I'll do myself egg and chips."

"I can do it for you," Stella says, her usual stubborn self.

He stubs out his cigarette. "No, Mum. You do yours and Dad's. I'll do my own when you've finished."

She gives him one of her looks. "I can do egg and chips, you know."

"I know, Mum," he says, going up behind her and tickling the back of her neck.

"Don't do that. You know I don't like it."

They're always getting at each other, those two, and true to form Stella can't leave it be. "I don't know why you have to wear that scruffy old jumper. Doesn't look as if it's seen the inside of a washing machine since you bought it."

"Spoiling for a fight, little Min?" Paul asks.

She whips off her apron and storms out of the kitchen. "How am I supposed to do a meal with you two under my feet? I'm going to have a soak. You can do dinner yourselves. I'm not hungry."

"Don't use up all the water," I shout after her. "I want a bath later."

"Go and sit down, Dad," Paul says. "I'll see to the stew."


## Valerie

"He's so set on it," Mum whispers down the phone. "He won't listen to reason."

"I've told you. Let him have it," I say, cool as Cruella De Vil.

It's not that I want him to die. I love him. He's my Dad, isn't he? And I do feel sorry for him. It must've been tough, being there on his own, finding those two golf balls and knowing if they aren't seen to, he'll cop it. It's the ten years that get me. A decade more life for him. The black cap for her. Where does her arthritis come from if it's not anger she's suppressed all these years, biting her tongue instead of telling the old sod what she thinks of him?

She says it's not worth it. "He'd make my life a misery."

"What about all the grief he's caused you?" I said one night when she was here last month. "What about the affairs?"

"They didn't matter," she said. "He kept them separate. He's always loved his family. We come first in his eyes."

If you love someone, you don't screw around. He didn't love her enough, that's what it boils down to. Bet he only stopped when he got found out or got too old for it.

But are they different from any other marriage? My first clear recollection of childhood is a row. Not my parents, my grandparents. We were standing on the pavement of the steep village street outside their terraced house in Carlin Howe, me up with them for a fortnight on my summer holidays, all dressed up in our Sunday best, even though it was only a Wednesday. I stood tall in my brand new Clarke's sandals buffed to a shine by Grandpa, white socks, green dress with red sash and a coat to keep out the stiff Yorkshire breeze that blew in off the coast straight to the coal tips. Each hand was locked in the grip of a grandparent.

"We'll go and get a proper lunch," my grandmother said. I liked the way she said 'proper', rolling the 'r'.

"Fish and chips," Grandpa said. "That's what we want."

"We're taking the bairn out for a treat," Grandma said, "and she needs proper food."

"Fish and chips is proper grub, woman. Good bit of Whitby cod. No finer food than that."

Her grip on my hand got tighter. "You've always been a cheapskate. You want to get away with spending as little as possible. I don't mind if it's me but I won't have it when the child's here."

I kept quiet and looked up at the sky. Seagulls were squawking above mountains of shiny coal. I tried to wriggle my hands free.

Grandpa released his grip for a second then clasped my wrist. Grandma held on.

"I just want to take the child somewhere she'll feel comfortable," Grandpa said. "Not one of those high falutin' places where you don't dare eat your peas off your knife. She'd love fish and chips, wouldn't you, pet?"

"No, she wouldn't," Grandma replied. "What the child wants is a proper lunch. Nice bit of roast beef with all the trimmings, ice-cream to follow."

She bent down and peered into my face. Her eyes were sparkling jet beads, a dewdrop glistened on the tip of her nose. "You want to come with me, don't you, chick?"

Grandpa let go of my hand. "Well, I'm off." He looked at me through his round, brown-framed glasses. "Are you coming with me?"

Grandma was still clinging on for dear life so I went with her. We took the bus to Middlesborough and went to Binns' department store. The roast beef was hard to cut and took forever to chew. I tried to make the ice-cream last but it wouldn't. We trudged round the store after lunch, looking for scratchy wool and buttons for the cardigan she was threatening to make me.

"It's fun shopping together, isn't it?"

When we got outside the store and were waiting for the bus, I was sick all over my new shoes.


I started learning then. Marriage is crap. For women, that is. I always knew it and now it's been scientifically proved. Men go to pieces when left, divorced or widowed.

Women Live Longer.

So in the interest of good health and longevity, I have decided never to engage in what is commonly called a relationship again. And what do I do when I feel like a bit of hurly burly? I call up one of the toy boys. A small but exclusive stable. Took a while to set up but now I think I've cracked it.

Six months after Max I put the first ad in a highbrow Zurich broadsheet. I'd decided I couldn't hit the sack with a man who didn't speak English, so said I was looking for an anglophile. I forgave Iso his name because, in contrast to the many gents who wrote that they 'were spoking english most fluentially,' he could spell and write an intelligible sentence. He looked old in his photo, older than my forty-ish, but he had a kind face and said he'd studied at Princeton.

I arranged to meet him in the bar of the Savoy in Zurich. First test. Would he moan about being somewhere decent, where your glass isn't decorated with the last drinker's lipstick? Passed, I thought smugly, as the escalator carried me up to the *Bahnhofstrasse*, where silver-coiffed *Damen*, backs bent double from the weight of their jewellery, rubbed their noses against designer windows. I strolled past jeweller's, jeweller's, chocolate shops and more jeweller's until I got to *Paradeplatz* and dived into the warm, chattering fug of the bar. A beautiful Richard-Gere grey smiled and raised an eyebrow. My God, I thought, my luck's in. Thank you, Lord. He didn't look a bit like his photo but I never recognise the old bag in mine. I started to push my way through the crowd, heart as light as a Michel Roux meringue, when something tugged at my sleeve.

"Valerie," a garlic voice whispered.

I spun round to give the idiot as much of a gobful as I could without drawing breath, and looked into an exact replica of the face in Iso's photo. Or rather, what the face would look like in twenty years' time. The handsome black hair on his head had migrated south and was now sprouting from his nose, his rustic cheeks sagged down to his collar.

"I'm so happy to see you," he said, clutching my elbow. "Might have missed each other in this crowd."

As he led me to a corner table that had just been vacated by a man in a banker's overcoat and an anorexic blonde, I told myself to get a grip. So he wasn't Richard Gere. So what? He was at least bright. He'd studied at Princeton, for God's sake.

"What would you like to drink?"

"A glass of champagne, please. I've had a tough day."

Not to mention the shock of a lifetime.

As I sat down, he leered at my legs. I picked up my raincoat and put it on my lap. "Bit chilly in here."

"We'll soon warm you up." A gold tooth glinted in each corner of his mouth.

"Tell me about your job. It sounds really interesting." He'd written that he 'was in a higher position at the Swiss national railways.' I'd pictured him sitting in a large office in Schlieren, the Swiss Crewe, from whence the SBB whizzed off to the mountains, nooks and crannies of *la belle Suisse*.

"Must be a really stressful job, being in charge of all those trains. I mean, how many people work for you? Hundreds? Thousands?"

"Well," he said, taking a sip of his herbal tea, "perhaps you got the wrong impression from my letter."

I frowned. "You said you had a very good job."

"I do. Excellent employers, the SBB."

"You said you were in a high position." I took a handful of the best salted almonds in Zurich. "You wrote you have a lot of problems with your staff."

"I do."

He stared at my boobs.

I pulled my jacket tight across my chest.

"How many people do work for you, then?" I fed the almonds into my mouth, steady as a conveyor belt.

He coughed. "One."

"Sorry," I said, raising my glass so the waitress could see I wanted a refill. "Couldn't hear you with all this noise. Thought you said 'one'."

"I did. I'm *Stationsvorstand* of the station in Niederbrünneli.

There are just the two of us, but it's a very important job. And Urs can be very trying at times."

"I'm sure," I muttered, resisting the urge to run. "Tell me about Princeton. I've always regretted going to a crap university. Wish I'd gone somewhere fantastic like you."

"Princeton's very nice," he nodded, smothering a covert belch with a grey hand. "But then Devon is a beautiful county, don't you think?"

He might have graduated from one of the best universities in the world but his geography was even worse than mine. "New England, you mean."

"No," he said. "Devon. Princeton in Devon. It's a lovely village and the evening course in English was most useful. Most useful indeed."

"*Fräulein*," he shouted to the waitress. "The bill, please."

Richard Gere flashed me a sympathetic smile, picked up his raincoat and left.

"Together or separate?" the waitress inquired.

"Separate," Iso said firmly. "I pay for the mineral water, the lady is paying for the champagne."


Then there was Giorgio, who had a country house in Tuscany, 'weez many beeautiful olivio trees in ze garden', which was obvious from the fact that he'd embalmed his head with most of their produce. I was getting seriously depressed. Before each date I'd tell myself it was only a couple of hours out of my life, but that insidious hope was always there, every time – that even though the chances were less than winning the lottery, I'd still come face to face with someone drop-dead gorgeous. The last straw was the letter from the Turkish gentleman who, misunderstanding the word 'anglophile', assured me he 'was verry interested for all sexual practisings.'

I dropped 'anglophile' from the next ad and decided to be more masculine in my approach. Say what I wanted; no frills, no fuss, no candyfloss illusions.

*Short-term relationship. Sex and fun essential. Absolutely No Commitment.*

It worked like a dream. None of them last longer than six months, top whack. If they start leaving their toothbrush in the bathroom and the old t-shirt they sleep in under the pillow, out they go. No pardon, no mercy. Exactly what the bastards do to us.

# Chapter Three

## November 1995

### Valerie

"Are you absolutely sure?" Wachtmeister Knoblauch asks for the tenth time.

"What do I have to do to convince you?" I shout. "The balcony door's open, there are thumping great footprints all over the bedroom carpet and my jewellery's gone."

"You didn't leave the door open?"

"I don't normally when I go away for the weekend."

"Where did you go?"

"London."

"Ah," he sighs. "I went to London once. Had a marvellous time I'll never forget walking round that big store. What's the name of it? Harrods, that's it. Now, you know, their food hall..."

It's half past one in the morning. My plane was two hours late, I was stopped on the motorway by a cop who fined me two hundred francs for speeding then told me to sleep well, my father's probably about to snuff it and I've been burgled. I do not want to chat about Harrods' sodding food hall. "Could you send someone round?"

"You're sure it can't wait until tomorrow morning?"

Mentally I gut, fillet and slice him. "I'll be at work. Can't you send them now?"

"I'll see what I can do."

I wonder what would happen if I was being stabbed to death. Would he ask for a lowdown on the knife? 'Swiss Army model, is it? Wonderful workmanship. Last forever. My son gave me one last Christmas.'

I pour myself half a pint of Glenfiddich and flop down on the sofa, a blob of shock and fury.

Mum phoned on Monday. "It's your Dad," she said, bursting into tears. "He caught a cold."

Christ Almighty, I thought. I know he's one of the great hypochondriacs but isn't this going a teensy bit far?

"We went up to the hospital for his check-up and Professor Macbeth said he couldn't do the op till your Dad feels better. He was so disappointed."

"So?" I might have been a bit curt. I was thinking of the tests I was going to mark before Eastenders – 3z's first attempt at grammar. From the few I'd glanced at, it looked as if they were living up to their name. "A cold's not fatal, for goodness' sake."

"It's turned to flu."

"But you both had the injection. You told me ages ago."

"I did but your Dad didn't."

I doodled on the pad next to the phone, a red circle getting smaller and smaller till there was just a wet blob.

"He's so weak," she sniffed. "I'm thinking of calling the doctor. He looks all feeble and helpless."

\*

On the plane, tests spread out on the fold-down table, I wondered if I was being too harsh. Should I be Swissly neutral in my parents' skirmishes? I'd placed myself so firmly on Mum's side ever since that Sunday in the lower sixth. She was at the sink, arms deep in a greasy mix of suds and gravy. I was flicking a tea-towel over a handful of spoons.

"Could I say I was going out with you?" she asked. "If I needed to." She wiped a hair out of an eye with a soggy wrist.

"Dunno. Where you going?"

Wild boar snores issued from the front room. Dad was asleep in front of the box. Paul was at the table cutting paths into congealed gravy with a lump of cold, grey beef. Mum had said he couldn't get down till he'd finished.

"Just out," she said airily. "With a friend."

I knew that shifty look. It was on my face often enough. Ewan and I had started doing it, on the front-room carpet on a Saturday night when my parents had hit the sack, more comfortably in my bed on Wednesday afternoon instead of Double Games. Dad couldn't know, I reasoned, but he glared at me as if he did.

"What kind of friend?"

Mum picked up a Brillo pad and attacked a saucepan.

"Just a friend. You know."

She took Dad's plate, walked over to the pedal bin and scraped thin slivers of fat onto potato peelings. "It's not what you think," she whispered. "We just talk. Sometimes he reads Shakespeare to me."

Crap, I thought. No one reads Shakespeare when they could be doing it. She just didn't want to admit it. That was ok with me, though. I understood. Admitting to sex at her age was disgusting. I'd be embarrassed, too.

"It's my driving instructor," she said.

So that was why she always changed and put on make-up before a lesson. I didn't know what to say. It was a novel situation, her asking me for something instead of dishing out commands.

We heard the ping of the telly switch and footsteps.

"Bloody awful match." Dad picked up a knife from the draining board. "This is still dirty."

He dropped it back in the water, splashing Mum's face. "Don't know why they got that new manager. Could do just as well myself."

He said that about everyone. My Dad, the BBC presenter. My Dad, the Olympic swimmer, the newspaper columnist, the county councillor, the Prime Minister.

My Dad, the bloody Queen.

"Why don't you, then?" I didn't bother to hide the sarcasm.

"When are you going for another of your so-called lessons, Minnie?" he said, ignoring me. Minnie, her middle name. He used it whenever he wanted to upset her – just about every day.

"Tomorrow."

"Don't know why you bother. You'll never learn. Far too old. In any case, you've got me to ferry you around."

"I'll see Ewan tomorrow night," I said, when he'd gone back to the telly. "Where shall we say we're going?"

So Mum went snogging with Romeo of the Three-Point-Turn and I covered her tracks. She went out with her fella, I went out with Ewan. Sometimes. Sometimes I went out with our next door neighbour, left-hand side. I'd always fancied him; slim, smily and extremely sexy even if he was going a bit thin on top. It started when I was babysitting for them. Robert'd chat about school while Maggie, his wife, got ready for bed. One day he was taking the kids swimming and he called out to Mum, asking if I wanted to go along.

I poked my head out of the bedroom window and said, "Yes, please. If you can squeeze me in."

He did.

## Jack

Eleven, twelve, thirteen. Thirteen beige leaves, three rows to a yard of wallpaper. Twelve square feet, that makes... Sod it. My brain's gone doolally along with the rest of me. The stairs creak and I call out, "What's the time?"

"Twenty minutes later than last time you asked," Stella says.

"I'm bored."

"I know you are, dear." She pokes her head round the bedroom door. "Why don't you read some of your new book?"

"Not in the mood." I gave up after I realised I'd read the same bloody sentence fifteen times.

"Then rest. You're poorly."

She comes up to the bed and starts faffing with the bedclothes, letting in a draught. "Leave me alone, woman, will you?"

"Would you like a cup of tea?"

"Yes, my throat's parched."

"I'll make you one of those herbal ones Paul brought. Peppermint, I think it is."

"No, you won't. I'll have PG Tips or nothing."

She goes downstairs and I hear her turn on the radio. It's after nine and she always listens to Radio Four so it's bound to be that Mervyn Bragg, big girl's blouse with his bouffant hair. She and Valerie think he's wonderful, God help them. The doorbell rings and I cheer up. That'll be Paul. He said he might pop in today. I'm just straightening my bedclothes, patting down my hair when the bedroom door opens and Dr Mathews walks in. She's in her thirties, a pretty girl, even if she does wear trousers. Flat shoes, too. It's a shame 'cos I'm sure as eggs is eggs that under that grotty blue denim there's a pair of cracking legs.

"Now, Mr Sterling," she smiles. "What's the trouble?"

"Not feeling too good, to tell you the truth."

"He's been terrible, doctor," Stella says. "Sweating one minute, freezing the next, falling all over the place."

"I can tell the doctor how I am. I haven't been struck dumb yet."

Stella marches out of the room, Dr Mathews gets out her stethoscope and listens to my chest. She takes my blood pressure, too. Very thorough, very professional. Says she's going to give me a course of antibiotics.

"Whatever you like, just as long as you get rid of this flu sharpish. I've got an important op coming up."

"I know that, Mr Sterling," she says. "Don't you worry. We'll have you fit as a fiddle in no time."

When she's gone, Stella comes up with a cup of tea.

"I don't know why you had to call her," I say.

"You're ill, that's why."

"I don't like you doing things behind my back. You should have asked me if I wanted the doctor or not."

"You'd have said no."

"Too right I would. There's nothing wrong with me that a day or two's rest won't cure."

"But you'll get better faster with the antibiotics."

"I know all that," I say, losing my rag. "But you have no right, no right at all to do things behind my back."

"Just drink your tea, will you?" she says, "before it gets cold."

I really fancy that cup of tea but I'll be damned if I'll drink it when she tells me to. "And don't boss me about," I shout. "I'm not bloody senile!"

She scoots out of the room and I don't see her for a couple of hours. Serves me right, I suppose, but I'm not decrepit yet and I won't be treated as if I am.

I'm looking at my fingernails, thinking I'll get Stella to bring the clippers and a file up next time she deigns to show her face, when I hear a key in the front door and Paul coughing and clearing his throat. There's a thud of boots and a, "Wotcha, Mum. What're you up to, apart from no good?"

Click goes the kettle. Good. I'll get my cup of tea.

"Don't know why you polish shoes," I hear him say. "It's a waste of time. Could be chilling out instead."

I don't know why she doesn't leave them. I'll be up and about in no time, as soon as those antibiotics start working. Then I'll do our shoes, just like I've always done. I pull myself up in bed and try to punch my pillow into shape. Bloody thing keeps going flat. I knew we should have got the better ones, not these foam things. When I'm feeling better, I'll go down to Fishpool's myself, get a pair of decent ones.

A couple of minutes later Paul walks in holding two mugs. "Good to see you." I raise my face for him to give me a kiss. Wouldn't let any other bloke kiss me. Not on your nelly, but with my Paul it's different.

"Are you taking some holiday?" It's Friday, at least I think it is. Perhaps he's decided to have a long weekend.

"No." He lights up a cigarette.

"But you're not sick?" He looks all right to me. He is a bit pale, but then getting up at four every morning's bound to take its toll.

"No."

"What's up, then? Haven't given you the sack, have they?"

"'Course not. I walked out this morning. Told them to stuff it."

"Bloody hell, son." I lift my mug carefully and take a sip. It scalds my lips so I put it back on the bedside table, sloshing a bit over the side. "Mop that up before your mother sees it, will you?"

He gets a clean handkerchief out of his pocket and clears up the mess. I think of saying hankies weren't meant for that but don't.

"Have you told your mother?"

He grins at me. "What do you think?"

"You'll have to tell her sometime."

The ash is hanging off the end of his fag. He sees me looking at it, gets up and goes to the bathroom to flush it down the bog. When he comes back, he sits on the side of the bed. "I'm not doing this to piss the two of you off, you know."

"I know it's not much of a job but Securicor'll never go bust and you'd have a decent pension."

"Back in a minute," he says. "Got to get something to eat. I'm starving."

He comes back with the biscuit tin and holds it out to me. I shake my head.

He takes a chocolate digestive, taps it on the edge of the box to get rid of the crumbs. "I couldn't take it, Dad. I hated it. Every minute of every day. If I'd stayed, I'd have gone round the bend."

"I understand that, son, but who's going to pay your rent? What about the gas, the electric?" He's working his way through the biscuits, slowly but steadily. "How are you going to pay for your food?"

He shrugs. "I've got enough to tide me over till I can sign on. The council'll pay my rent. I'll be all right."

I pick up the mug again, blow on my tea. I'm not going to make things worse by having a go. I'll leave that to his mother.

"What are you going to do?"

"I'm looking round." He finishes his tea and puts the lid back on the empty box. "I've got the local paper and there are some ads in The Big Issue. I'll find something. Better go and have a word with Mum."

I tell myself not to worry, at thirty-five he's old enough to look after himself but I know I will. I think he's being rash, chucking it in without anything to go to. If he had a wife and kiddies, he wouldn't be able to.

I've only been out of work once but by God, I'll never forget the feeling. It was back in the early days. We'd only been married six years or so. Valerie must have been about four. We were still living at my parents'. Mum hadn't sold up after my father's death. I was fed up that we couldn't afford a place of our own, not even on both our wages, but there was no way we could have scraped the money together for a deposit.

Stella must have realised something was wrong from the look on my face as I walked through the door. She was sitting with my mother, the china horse Mum had bought Valerie on the dining table between them. Mum had gone on one spending spree after another since Dad died, not that I blamed her. Always kept her short of cash, the miserable git. He'd even buy her clothes. She'd taken Valerie up to Selfridges the day before, much to Stella's disapproval, bought her two coats, four dresses and the horse. It was a beautiful thing, about ten inches high. It stood looking down its long, white muzzle in a snooty sort of way. Valerie loved it. She'd taken it to bed with her the night before and one of the back legs had snapped off.

Stella was saying, "I'm all right. Just give me the glue. It's a clean break." But Mum wouldn't hear of it.

"There are splinters all over the place," she said. "You'll see the join a mile off."

Valerie ran over and tugged at the hem of my coat. "I want my horse."

"I know, love." I picked her up and marched straight to the sideboard, sat her on top and poured myself a double Scotch.

Mum pursed her lips. "Not setting a very good example."

"What on earth's the matter?" Stella said.

There's no point putting it off, I thought. "Pettifer called me into the office today."

I picked Valerie up, carried her and the Scotch to our usual chair. She rested her head on my chest and I ruffled her hair. "Havisham's sold out to the Co-op."

"Things are going to pot," Mum said. "You mark my words. It's the beginning of the end."

"Oh, Jack." Stella reached across the table and gave my hand a squeeze.

I wanted something to do so I took the horse, upended it and smeared a thick layer of glue on the cut-off point. "I'm not surprised. Rumour's been doing the rounds for months."

It was one of those old-fashioned stores, the sort that snuffed it years ago and good bloody riddance. Wooden floors, dark showcases and metal cash capsules that whirred on overhead wires to the cashiers, who sat in the middle of the sales floor. I'd been floorwalker for five years, doing my job but refusing to kowtow to management. Should have arselicked my way up the ladder like the other gits then I might have been kept on. But it was too late for all that now.

I took the severed leg and pressed it firmly against the join. "They won't be needing any floorwalkers. We've all got the sack. Two weeks' pay and our cards."

"Horse," Valerie muttered into my shirt front. "I want my horse."

I kissed the top of her head and put the horse on its side. The bloody leg wilted away from the join, leaving a trail of glue on the newspaper.

"What on earth are we going to do?" Stella said. She'd gone so pale it made me feel worse than I did already.

I said the same as Paul. "I've got the paper. I'm looking."

"Paper," Valerie whispered. "Read the paper."

Stella's cheeks were going red. "What are we going to do about money? My Mum and Dad can't help. They've only got their bit of pension."

Valerie grabbed my tie and pulled my face down to hers. I felt her breath on my cheeks. "What's a pension?"

I set her gently on the floor. "Tell you later, poppet. Let me talk to Mummy now."

"I've got a tidy sum," Mum broke in. "Your father was a good saver."

"No," I said. "I'm not taking anything of his."

"Now, hold on just one minute," Stella said. "That's very generous. Thank you."

Valerie had picked up the horse and was walking it and the broken-off leg, one in each hand, across the table. "Pension," she droned. "Pension. Only got a bit of pension."

Mum frowned and struggled to her feet. For the first time I thought how frail she looked; shrunk, somehow caved in. She and Dad had hated each other but since his death she'd seemed smaller, diminished in a way. She took the horse, laid it back on the newspaper then got hold of Valerie's hand. "We'll be in the garden," she said.

"No need, Mum. The answer's no."

Stella said nothing until they'd left the room but I could sense her anger under the surface. "What do you think you're doing?" she shouted. "Take the money, for our sake if not for your own."

She jammed the top on the glue and a thick blob oozed down the side onto her fingers.

I took a clean handkerchief out of my pocket and held it out to her. She shook her head and tried to wipe the glue onto the newspaper. All she did was coat her fingers with newsprint and tiny shards of china.

"You can say what you like but I'm not taking anything from my father."

"Rather see us starve, would you?"

"Don't be ridiculous."

I got up, went over to her and grabbed hold of her sticky hands. "I said I'd get a job and I will."

I picked up the handkerchief to wipe her hands but she wrenched it away.

"The trouble with you," she said, "is you're too rotten proud. If my Dad offered me money, I'd take it."

"If it were your Dad," I said, "I would take it."

"I'll never understand you, Jack Sterling," she said, shoving the horse, leg and glue at me. "Now fix that if you're so clever."

She got up and ran downstairs, out into the garden. I could hear her talking to Mum, her voice raised, but I didn't go to the window. I didn't want to hear what she was saying. When they came back in, I'd poured myself another Scotch and was messing around with the horse. Got the leg back on in the end. The join wasn't visible if you didn't look closely but the leg was shorter than before. I kept fiddling with the bloody thing all night but however hard I tried I couldn't make it stand up straight.

"Are you staying for something to eat?" I say when Paul comes up to collect my mug.

"Yep. Looks like it."

"Be nice for your Mum to have some company. What about your football, though? You won't be going to White Hart Lane if you're on the dole." Not the price tickets are today. Daylight robbery.

"I can go with John when he's got a spare ticket."

"Good," I said. "I'm glad to know you've got good mates."

As he walks out of the room, I see that one of his back pockets is hanging off. And they're frayed round the ankles, his jeans. Even without my glasses I can see a couple of holes in the backside. There's no point telling him to get another pair now. Just have to slip him the cash.

Stupid thing happens when I'm talking to him after dinner. I've had mine on a tray in bed. Didn't feel like getting up. We're chatting away and I call Paul Gordon. God knows why. He's not the same build at all. Gordon was short and wiry like Mum's side of the family. Paul's tall like me. No bloody resemblance. It must be his tone of voice that puts me in mind of my brother. I'm taking the piss out of Spurs, never a hard thing to do, 'specially at the moment with that clown Gerry Francis. Worst thing they ever did, making him manager. Not got what it takes to run a Premier League side. He won't last long. I've told Paul. Be out on his ear in next to no time.

"Look what your lot's come to," I say. "Bloody idiot for a manager and no decent players. No wonder you're crap."

He nicks one of my fags and lights up. "Talking out of your arse."

If I had my eyes closed, I'd think it was Gordon. That's what he'd say when I rubbed him up the wrong way.

"You're a daft little bugger, son," I say. At least that's what I mean.

"What did you call me?" Paul opens the window and flicks ash outside. I think of having a smoke then decide against it. Wouldn't be worth the aggro.

"You been at the Famous Grouse again, Dad?"

"What are you talking about?" I've had enough of Stella treating me like an old fool, let alone my kids doing the same.

"You called me Gordon."

"No, I didn't."

"You did."

We go on like that for a bit. "Did I really?"

He nods.

"Suppose I must have done, then." He wouldn't lie to me. Not my Paul.

I have been thinking about Gordon lately. Must be Remembrance Sunday. Stella has it on the radio, Christ knows why. I won't let her turn on the telly. Won't bloody watch it, not now, not ever.

### Valerie

"I'm tired, Valerie," Dad says when I walk into the bedroom. "Knackered." He's stretching a stick-insect arm towards me, the first show of affection for a long time.

I perch on the bed and the marshmallow mattress tilts him towards me. "You're going to be fine."

I'm lying through my teeth. God knows how much weight he's lost since August. In three months he's shrunk to half his size. I had a tall, strong Dad in summer. Where the hell has he gone?

He closes his eyes. The lids are mottled, baggy. Too big for what they cover.

I don't want to leave him on his own but there's no point watching him sleep so I have a cup of low-cal chocolate with Mum then get to bed. I'm sorry he's ill but glad I'm there. Happy in a weird sort of way that he needs me.

Should have known it wouldn't last.

I pop in to see him as soon as I get up. "Must be bored on your own, Dad. Shall I sit with you for a while?"

He smiles. A tired, old turtle smile. "No, dear. Don't bother. Don't want to keep you."

Keep me from what? I'm only damn well here because of you. No, that's not true. I'm here because of Mum. If she wants family solidarity, I'll deliver.

"When's Paul coming?"

"Later in the morning, I think Mum said. I'll go and ask."

I stomp downstairs, snip Melvyn Bragg in his prime and ping on the kettle. "He's asking for Paul."

"He does all the time," she says. "Doesn't seem to want me." She laughs – an apologetic giggle.

"Or me."

She gives me a hug. "I'm sure that's not true, dear."

"Want a chocolate Hobnob?"

"Why not?" she says. "Let's go mad."


### Jack


Wish I could have picked her up at the airport. That's always been my job. Don't like the thought of her travelling all that way on the Tube. Not at night. And it's my only chance to have her to myself. Many's the time we've missed the turn-off from the M25, I've been yacking so much. Once she's back here, she and her mother are holed up in the kitchen. I go out sometimes to see what they're chatting about, but they stop more often than not.

Mustn't worry, though. When I've had my operation, I'll be my old self, or even better. I'll be back in my own bed for a start, depriving Stella of sleep. And during the day I'll be up the library reading the papers and chatting up the girls who order my books.

"You ought to work here," Julie said a while ago. "You know as much about books as I do."

"Now, don't go giving me that old toffee," I said. "You want my daughter for that. Studied it, you know. Not English literature, not her first degree. That was German and French, but still."

"How is your daughter, Jack?"

She's a nice girl, that Julie. Always asks about the family. "She's fine," I said. At least I think she is. That's what she says in her letters.


## Valerie

Paul arrives at eleven.

"Is that my Paul?"

We leave them to it. Mum and I go shopping down the Cross, then do lunch. I give Paul a break for half an hour in the afternoon. He's got cramp in his legs and a stiff back. But when I go to sit with Dad, the old bugger panics.

"You're not going now, Paul, are you?" he whispers.

"No, Dad. Just going for a pee, something to eat and a fag. You can talk to Val."

I sit and look at the photos on Mum's dressing table; me and Paul as woolly babes, spiky nine-year-olds, porridge-faced teenagers. None of Mum and Dad, not even of their wedding. Now and again our eyes meet and Dad and I give each other weak, embarrassed smiles. Like strangers on a train.

I fish a paperback out from among the syrups, tissues and assorted tablets on his bedside table. "What's this?"

"Ken Travis' latest. Borrow it if you like."

I hate war novels, only let a kid read Hemingway for their orals if they refuse everything else, but it wouldn't be right to row with him now.

I open the book and sigh with relief. "Can't. It's a library book. Don't want you getting into trouble."

"They won't mind, dear," he says. "I'm up there so often I get special treatment. You take it and enjoy it."

We have a bad night. Mum sleeps in their bed, I take the boxroom. I tell her to shut the door and have a decent rest. I'll keep mine open and listen in case Dad needs anything. I tell him to stay in bed. He isn't strong enough to get up on his own.

I wake in a white flash of shock, wondering where I am.

"Val," a voice wheezes from the landing.

I told you to stay in bed, I think. You difficult old git. "Are you all right?" I scramble out of bed as fast as I can.

"No."

I get to the landing just in time to see him fall. He clings to the frame of the bathroom door, fingers slipping on the paint. I dash forward but can't save him. Thud, he goes, like a sack of old logs. Thud and crack, hitting his head on the skirting board.

"Oh, my poor Daddy."

The words just burst out. I must be half asleep.

He's cut his forehead. Nothing serious but enough to smear the woodwork red. He can't get up on his own so I drag him back to bed, prop him up against the bedstead and push his knees up to his chest. I just about manage to heave him back between the sheets. I scrabble through the bathroom cabinet and find a packet of plasters. I take the biggest, wet a flannel with warm water and clean him up. His skin puckers under the adhesive like an elephant's bum.

He falls three more times during the night. Once out of bed, once by his bedroom door, once in the bathroom, his head just missing the airing cupboard. He calls out every time. I never manage to save him.

\*

The two Swiss Plods turn out to be quite yummy. Blue eyes, pink choochy cheeks from the cold. One Lindt-finest dark, one

Gruyère blond. Pert bums, I notice, when they take off their parkas.

"We always work together," the blond one says.

Pinky and Perky.

When I show them the black footprints that cover the bedroom carpet, they nod knowingly at each other.

"Yeees," Pinky says, removing a tape measure from a case and sizing up the prints as carefully as a court shoemaker. "Forty-one. We've seen these before."

"Oh, good. You'll get the bastard."

Perky examines the door handle then dusts the window pane with white powder. "What we mean by that," he qualifies, "is that we've seen his footprints a number of times. We don't know who he is, though."

Great. All they have to do is comb the country for a bloke who wears size forty-one Timberlands.

"Our guess is," Pinky explains, "he's Italian and just popped over the border to do a bit of pre-Christmas shopping."

"So you don't think I'll get my jewellery back?" It's a rhetorical question. I know damn well what the answer is.

"Well," admits Perky, putting powder and brush back in the case. "The chances are pretty slim. This guy really is a professional."

His tone is one of admiration.

When they've gone, I open my wardrobe and clear every shelf of bras, knickers, tights, stockings. I'll wash them in the morning. I flaunt apartment etiquette by hoovering up footprints at two a.m. but still can't sleep in my bedroom so stumble down to the cellar, drag up the old mattress I've been meaning to chuck and make up a bed in the study. I keep the telly on all night, that and every light in the flat. Blackpool illuminations in *Walchwil am See*.

I finish the whisky and lie down on the mattress, keeping the door open, my eyes fixed on the balcony. Just in case the burglar comes back, though Pinky and Perky assured me he wouldn't.

"They never do," they chorused, identical smiles on their shiny, fresh faces.

What do they know, I think, swaying off to the loo and bashing my elbow on the door frame. Can't even bloody well catch the bugger.

Two hours later I'm still wide awake so take Dad's book out of my bag. *The Silent Battlefield.* The cover is an arid stretch of rock, one still-smoking bush slightly off centre. I shake my head, throw the book on the floor. Sorry, Dad. Can't read this crap. I reach down into the bag and find 3z's well-travelled tests. Might as well do something useful if I'm not going to get any sleep. Exercise 1 (synonyms) is ok. They might not be so bad, after all. Maybe they just didn't get on with last year's teacher. Exercise 2, transforming verbs into nouns is worse but acceptable – ticks still outnumber crosses. When I start on the translation, I groan. A few are good, some bear a passing resemblance to English, the majority might have been spewed from a randomly-programmed computer. We practised forever, you little buggers, I think, red-ringing eight words out of ten on each line. I gave you extra translations, every exercise I could find. We went through the grammar till a chimp with half a brain cell could have done the test in his sleep. Well, you're not getting away with it. You're not going to give me crap work and be rewarded. You are going to pay.

We all do. When I give the tests back, three burst into tears and one rips up the test sheet and shouts that he'll never, ever do any work for English again. It's a shitty language, he doesn't want to learn it anyway. He spent five hours the night before learning vocab and grammar. He could have been playing computer games.

"But I told you how to learn. We spent the first week of term looking at the best ways of revising, remember?"

He grunts.

"When did you start?"

"Just told you," he says, wiping snot and tears on his Calvin Klein sweatshirt. "Night before the test. I worked from nine till two in the morning. Waste of rotten time."

"You've got to start earlier. Split up the vocab, learn in palatable chunks. You know all that."

"Didn't have time."

I take a deep breath, count to ten and ask him to do his corrections.

He gets a calculator out of his rucksack and works out his average. "Shit!"

"Would you get on with your corrections, please? And I'd be grateful if you didn't use language like that in my classroom."

He mutters something unintelligible.

Grateful I didn't hear and therefore don't have to punish him, I turn away. When I turn back, he's doodling in his textbook. "I've asked you twice politely," I say. "Now I'm telling you. Do some work and stop wasting time."

He throws his book on the floor. "English is shit," he shouts. "I hate it."

"Then get out!" I shout back. "You can come back tomorrow morning and repeat the lesson. And don't even think of skiving because if you do, you'll be on Saturday morning detention for the rest of this term."

Tears stream down his face as he crawls under the desk to retrieve his book. He packs his rucksack with maximum noise and leaves. He doesn't quite dare to slam the door. The rest of the lesson is coffin-quiet, the kids cowering over corrections. When I walk into the staffroom to have a good whinge, Geoff, my old mate from uni, now Head of English, asks the culprit's name.

"Markus Rothenbühler," I say with Ted Heath's affection for Margaret Thatcher.

"He was just as bad when I taught him," Geoff says. "Did you know his dad died a month ago? Won't talk about it, though. That's why he cries at the slightest thing."

Gianni, prettiest of the toy boys, comes round that night. Italians are so helpful. Do anything for you at the drop of a cappuccino. Apart from being as sexy as the numbers he plays on his tenor sax, he's a whiz with a screwdriver. A real handy man. That's how we met. I had some pictures that needed hanging and a stereo I couldn't set up – odd jobs I didn't want to rely on my neighbours for. Like cockroaches, neighbours. Get them in your place once, you never get rid of them.

Gianni fits three new locks on the front door, one each on all the windows. If the burglar returns, at least he'll have to work to get in.

"What you could do," I say, "is wire up the balcony railing. That'd teach him he wasn't put into this world for pleasure alone."

"No can do, *cara*. You're allowed to protect your premises but not at the risk of injuring someone."

"So some swine can break into my flat and trash the place but if I try to stop him, I'm breaking the law?"

"*Eh, si – cara mia.*"

"Thank God we live in a free country."

He puts down the screwdriver. "Come here. Let me take your mind off things."

Floating on a post-coital cloud, I'm vaguely aware of the phone ringing. I totter out to the living room, hoping Gianni's not watching my middle-aged bum wobble, and pick up the receiver. "Yes?"

"It's only me," says a familiar voice. "Not disturbing anything, am I?"

My guts contract, hairs on arms and legs stand to attention.

"Haven't seen you for ages," says Max. "We've got such different timetables this year. Thought you might fancy a drink tomorrow after school."

"Oh, er, right."

"Same place, same time?"

"Yep."

I replace the receiver, do a little jig and stroll nonchalantly into the bedroom.

"I don't know why you can't give me a key," Gianni groans next morning when I haul him out of bed at six-thirty. "I'd put it in your mailbox when I leave. It's not as if I'd go through your stuff."

I shrug and stroke his stubbly face.

"Pick you up at six, then," he says. There's an edge to his voice but I refuse to notice it. No discussions, no explanations, those are the rules.

He runs his hands through shiny liquorice locks and yawns. "Angelo Branduardi. The concert in Zurich."

"Can't, I'm sorry." I give him the sexiest kiss I can manage at such an ungodly hour. "Something's come up."

After school I shower, tip half a bottle of Dolce and Gabbana down my cleavage and drive off to meet Max. The second I saw him in the staffroom on that first day of term, I knew I had to have him. He was a walking, talking Black Beauty. Eyes like sable-lashed honey pots were set in the kind of face that always has a smile just below the surface. His arms were maple syrup with a dusting of jet hair matching the curls that framed his face. He had pianist's hands – perfect for performing arpeggios on all my sharps and flats. With every breath he oozed vitality, sex, excitement.

I just about stopped myself from swooning.

Having ogled the goods, I took in the wrapping, which was classy, understated American. Very Ivy League. Navy blazer, white, open-necked shirt, chinos, no socks. I imagined him at Harvard, strolling under golden boughs on his way to a brilliant lecture. He was everything I'd ever dreamt of. Absolutely bloody perfect. I sashayed over to him, hips in a Monroesque wiggle. "I'm Val. I teach English."

"Name's Max. New boy in the department. It's my first job."

I glanced at his left hand. No ring. Good. I didn't think of the gold band on my own finger or of the man who put it there. Not even for a nano-second.

Two days later we were sitting down by the lake with Geoff. Ever since he'd got me the job in Zug, we'd gone drinking each Wednesday after school. He'd forsaken his usual pint and was sharing a litre of strawberry-pink rosé with Max and me. Max and I were feeding Geoff's crisps to the swans. He was getting his own back by making lewd gestures every time Max looked away. I'd told Geoff about my secret passion. I had to. I'd have burst otherwise.

"Val tells me you did Russian as your first subsid." Geoff arched one eyebrow in my direction.

"Yeah. Really got into it during my year in the States. Fascinating language. Wonderful literature."

"Val's always wanted to do Russian, haven't you, petal?"

I went borsch-red and kicked Geoff under the table.

"Really?" Max beamed his zillion-watt smile and my guts melted like sorbet in the sun.

"I have, actually," I lied. I'd have enrolled for Advanced Bog Cleaning if it'd got me closer to him.

"What about you, Geoff?" Max inquired. "Feel like having a go?"

"'Course he will," I said. "He'd love to."

Max raised his glass. "That's settled, then. I'll order the books and we can start next week."

"Are you sure you've got the time?" Geoff asked, hoping against hope.

"You two have been so good to me," Max smiled. "How could I possibly refuse?"

"Happy now?" Geoff and I had walked Max back to the station. He lived in Zurich with his mum and dad. Geoff said that was a bad sign. Wouldn't stand on his own two feet, but I understood. Why pay for a flat when you can live rent-free?

I nodded. Learning Russian meant I'd see Max the Marvellous six days a week.

"Be careful, though," Geoff frowned. "We don't want a Swiss *Anna Karenina*."

I gave him a bear hug and walked home, full of pity. Such a good bloke but so tragically cautious. Old before his time.

Our books were mustard yellow with blotchy print that looked as if it'd come off the page if we rubbed it. (Geoff tried and it did). Hunched over them, we struggled with the Cyrillic alphabet. I traced the letters of my name, tongue poking out of the corner of my mouth. BAM – that's who I was in our Russian lessons – not married, no ties so no need to feel guilty.

Max looked over our shoulders, nodding and murmuring encouragement. He leant down, chin centimetres from the nape of my neck. If I moved, his lips would brush it. I didn't. I was content to soak up his aftershave, feel his breath on my skin, tingle at every flash of lust that sizzled and sparked between us.

"I'll have to give you some homework," he said at the end of the lesson.

Geoff groaned.

Oh yes, please, sir, I thought. As much as you like and more.

*

"You need a break," I told Klaus Maria at dinner one February evening. "Why don't you go to Grindelwald?"

"That's a good idea. Sports holidays coming up."

"I didn't exactly mean the two of us."

Blue eyes clouded over. "Oh?"

"There's loads I need to do for school and you know I don't like ski-ing. I only come to keep you company."

That much at least was true. I loathed the diver's boots that made you walk like Frankenstein, the icy pistes that meant you fell bum over boobs sixty times an hour, the long, elbow-digging queues for the lifts, the even longer queues for the pleasure of eating bright orange, chemical sausage and potato salad that looked as if it had been pre-digested by a sick St Bernard.

"I suppose you're right," my husband said, sweeping his thick blond fringe from his forehead. "I haven't been once this season. Will you be all right on your own?"

"'Course."

I felt a brief twinge of guilt but not enough to stop me.

By the time the weekend arrived, he had a terrible cold. "I don't know if there's any point," he croaked. "I'm not going to do much ski-ing if I feel like this."

"You've booked now. Be a shame to lose the deposit."

I'd spent a fortnight sieving my recipe books, deciding what I was going to cook for Max. I'd had my eyelashes tinted, done a hundred sit-ups a day. I'd painted my toenails scarlet in the middle of winter, for God's sake! He had to go.

The town of Zug lies deep in pea-soupers from November to March, a detail I failed to consider when I jumped out of bed at 6 a.m. on D-Day. I showered, washed my hair and put on knock-him-dead war paint, thinking I was saving time for later. Then I tottered down through the fog to make sure I was the deli's first customer.

When I saw myself in the mirror behind the cheese counter, I yelped like a Chihuahua beneath a size-twelve boot. My hair, blow-dried to perfection, had slumped to straggles of pond weed. I scuttled out of the shop into the butcher's, praying I wouldn't see anyone I knew.

"*Gruezi, Frau Bumbacher,*" two mums and a gaggle of pupils chimed.

I looked straight ahead, pulled up my collar and pretended to be deaf.

By the time I'd done the shopping, fatigue was setting in. I trudged up the hill, only to find I'd forgotten the champagne. The deli said they'd deliver but charge twenty francs for the privilege. I told them I'd pick it up myself.

I sealed the beef, coated it with truffle pâté, wrapped it in pastry, threw away two thirds of a lettuce, washed the rest, then slumped down on the sofa for a mini-break. I woke up three hours later. In the bathroom I discovered my eye make-up was now doubling as blusher and the sofa cushion had left an unusual criss-cross pattern on my left cheek. I got a taxi to town to pick up the champagne then spent three hours reshowering, hairwashing and renovating.

What the hell was I going to wear? Trousers were definitely out, so was anything long. The best option was the size-ten bumfreezer I'd bought in the January sale – the one I'd been meaning to slim into. I managed to do it up but it sliced into my waist like the deli's salami cutter, so I settled for safe, size-twelve black. Not as sexy as I'd planned but actions would just have to speak louder than thighs.

After fifteen minutes' tussle with a python masquerading as a suspender belt, I pulled on my best black stockings, deftly putting a fist through both legs. I glanced at my watch and wailed. Only half an hour to go!

A taxi whizzed me to town for new stockings, which, as the shop only sold Fogal, cost a hundred francs a pair. I asked the driver if he had a lot of runs like this. He said no.

I arrived home panting and jittery. The lift was out of action so I had to take the stairs. I dragged on my clothes and just had time to arrange myself on the couch with a copy of *War and Peace*, open near the end, when the bell rang.

He stood there smiling, looking as edible as *Sprüngli's* best truffles. "Done much today?" he asked.

"Nah. Just hung around."

"Thought I'd bring a bottle of wine." He followed me into the kitchen. "Something smells good."

Our fingers touched as he took the corkscrew out of my hand.

We started with ceps sautéed in butter, brandy and herbs, then moved on to Beef Wellington and side salad.

We spoke little but leered a lot.

"That was the best meal I've ever had," he said, leaning back in his chair.

"I didn't do dessert."

"Good."

We moved to the sofa, where we devoted two minutes to the smallest of talk, then pounced on each other like lions on a sleeping gazelle. The bedroom was too far away, the floor would have to do, which it did nicely, then and every afternoon till Klaus Maria came home.

"But why move out, darling?" Klaus Maria asked. "We're so happy."

It wasn't real, though. Not anymore. It was like Mother's Pride – hygienic, hermetically sealed but no taste, no bite, no substance.

I didn't have the heart to tell him the truth. I was a bitch, I reasoned, not a sadist.

I stuttered the usual clichés – we'd grown apart, had nothing in common, ending up with, "I just have to go."

"I'll help you move," he said finally. "Just let me know when."

He went out, maybe for a walk, maybe to the office.

I felt guilty as hell, the lowest of the low. But not for one second did I think of staying.

Within weeks I'd seen a solicitor and shed five frumpish kilos. I felt alive for the first time in years, buzzing and bouncing for joy. I was no longer homesick. How could I be? The man I'd been waiting for all my life was there with me.

"You didn't move out because of me, I hope?" Max asked, one multiorgasmic evening.

"We hadn't been getting on for a while. It would have happened anyway."

Liar, liar, knickers on fire.

My Darling hadn't quite finished his degree. He was writing a thesis on Byron and I was doing the proofreading.

"You're a great help, you know." He cupped my face in his hands, bent down for a goodnight kiss.

I hated him going but knew he had to. He didn't want his parents to find out about us. They were Catholic, they wouldn't understand. And then there was Anita, the official girlfriend. I was jealous as hell but I saw him more than she did. Swiss schools were open six days a week so every day except Sundays he was mine.

I knew what Mum would say so didn't tell her. I'd got my fingers seriously frazzled with Dick, the married chemist I'd worked for on Saturdays while at school. But with Max it was different. For a start, he and Anita weren't married. They'd met just before he went to university. I knew he thought a lot of her but she wasn't on his intellectual level. And if he were that happy with her, why did he need me? She taught Home Economics, for Christ's sake. What did they have to talk about? The best recipe for *Rösti*?

We were sitting at a staffroom desk one day, playing footsie. It was half past four, the rest of the department had gone home, leaving us forty minutes of bliss before the cleaners arrived. I suggested going back to my place but he wouldn't.

"We'd end up in bed," he said, flashing topaz eyes.

He'd marked twenty essays, I'd had the same test sheet in front of me for the past half hour. What the hell had I been doing all my life, I wondered? I whiled away free periods doodling his name, counted every minute of the weekends he spent with Cookie Lookie. I refused to call her by her real name, kept her firmly two-dimensional. Definitely not 3D, most certainly not someone I might like.

He pencilled in a mark at the bottom of an essay, I drew a heart on the desk and for the thousandth time imagined what Fanny Von Craddock looked like. Short, my darling said, so I pictured a dwarf. Slim, he said. Good – no tits. Her hair was long, brown and thick (I'd brushed it off his jacket more than enough times), so I consoled myself by giving her a moustache. I knew I had to be patient, give him time to realise it was me he wanted. So I smiled, helped, supported – and gave him the screw of his life every Friday afternoon.

Something for the weekend.

I wanted to be better in bed, cook better, be wittier, brighter, totally irresistible. I wanted to outshine that woman in every single way.

He slipped the essays into his briefcase. "Penny for them."

"Nothing. Finished?"

"Yep, I'll have to be off."

"I'm nearly finished." Nineteen tests to go but I wasn't telling him. "Going out for our usual drink?" If he wouldn't come to my place, at least I could lust after him at our local.

"Can't."

"But we always go out after school."

"Have to go somewhere."

"Where?"

He sighed. "You don't want to know."

"Yes, I do." There was nothing I didn't want to know about my darling.

"It's Anita's birthday. Ok?"

No, it bloody well was not. Why couldn't she celebrate with other people? Go out with her mum and dad, for Christ's sake.

I shrugged, not bothering to hide my disappointment. I was going to make it as difficult for him as I could.

He lit a cigarette, clicked the lighter shut and threw it into his case. Another sign. "You're all right, aren't you?"

"Of course."

"See you tomorrow, then." He got up, stroked my shoulder. "I don't know what I'd do without you. You know that, don't you?"

I watched him walk out of the room, whistling softly, swinging his briefcase.

What was I worried about? He couldn't do without me. He'd just said so, hadn't he?

*

"So, what do you want to tell me, darling?" I poured another glass of champagne and kissed the tip of his gorgeous little hooter. I was dressed up in the slinky black number he liked; high heels, stockings, no knickers. He'd told me we had to talk. There was something important he had to say.

Golden eyes glittered in the candlelight and I knew what it was. He was leaving Action Woman. I was going to be promoted from the Bit on the Side to Number One. He would take me home to meet Mum and Dad, who'd be captivated. This time I'd be the perfect daughter-in-law.

"It's a bit difficult," he said, downing the champagne in one. Didn't like talking about his feelings, my poor darling.

I stroked his hand. "Come on, spit it out."

He examined the bows on his brand new sneakers. "I'm getting married."

Time stood still. I was flash frozen like a shrimp on a Cape Cod trawler.

"It's always been on the cards. We've been together a long time. I've always been honest with you, haven't I?" He patted my hand like a teacher saying sorry but you're not getting the book prize. Someone else was better.

"But.... but you love me," I stuttered.

At the most important moment in my life I came out with a bloody cliché. And to make it even worse, I fainted. I slid to the floor in slow motion, the world closed down and when I opened my eyes, he was leaning over me.

He helped me to my feet. "You're all right, aren't you? Strong as an ox, my Val."

"Yes, of course."

"And you'll be ok?"

"Yes."

"I do like you, you know. Very much. But I don't love you."

He coughed and grinned, embarrassment incarnate, then went off to plan his wedding with Spiderwoman.

"Sorry," I say to the gearbox and drive into the car park of our lakeside haunt. Max is married, our chapter's over. I long since gave up being angry with him. I squint in the mirror, give the warpaint one final check, spray a cloud of Chanel over my head so She can smell he's been out with a woman, and march off to do battle.

## Jack

"Don't put any of that peel stuff in, will you?" I tell Stella. We're out in the kitchen, me sitting on a stool, her doing the Christmas puddings. A bit late this year, but then we've got all behind, what with me being ill.

She stops stirring and gives me one of her looks. "How many years have I been making them?"

"What's that got to do with anything?"

"Nearly fifty years," Stella says. "I never put peel in because I know you don't like it. You tell me every year."

"No need to get shirty." I take a slurp of my tea. "What's up with you?" I wonder if it's her hormones then remember she got rid of all that years ago, thank Christ.

"Nothing you need worry about," she says, dipping my mother's silver tablespoon into the treacle, then twisting it so the brown blob doesn't drop on the Formica.

"So there is something?" I take a plate out of the cupboard by the sink and put it down on the work surface. "Rest the spoon on that. It'll make less of a mess."

She scrapes the treacle from the spoon and drops it into the washing-up bowl, ignoring the plate. There's no helping some people, they're so cussed.

"Will you promise not to get upset if I tell you?" she asks.

"I'll get upset if you don't."

She sighs. "Well, it's just that Valerie's been burgled."

"What?" I wish I was there in that bloody country. I'd go out and find the swine, make them wish they'd never been born.

"The night she flew back from here," Stella says. "Realised as soon as she walked through the door. Took all her jewellery and some cash. Didn't rubbish the place, though, so that's something, I suppose."

"Why the hell didn't you tell me?"

"Because you're still not well. We thought it better for you not to know."

"You didn't tell Paul. He wouldn't keep it from me."

"Come and sit in the other room," she says, taking my arm. "You've gone all pale. I did ask Paul and he agreed with Val and me."

I let her lead me into the living room and set me in my chair.

"Will you be all right for a minute," she asks, "while I finish up in the kitchen?"

I sit there in the dark, not bothering to turn on the light, wondering how I'd feel if someone broke into my home. It's all my fault, I keep thinking, all my bloody fault. If Valerie hadn't come home to see me, she wouldn't have been burgled.

# Chapter Four

## December 1995

### Valerie

"Sort yourselves out, you bastards," I hiss at the spaghetti swirl of fairy lights. If they were put away properly, we wouldn't have this performance. But that would be asking too much. Nothing's ever done right in this house.

Dad's in his armchair, watching every move.

"I thought we weren't bothering with all that." He looks pathetic, as pale as raw turkey, but I won't feel sorry for him. He's trying to ruin my Christmas and I'm not going to let him.

I chuck the lights back in their box. I'll go down to Boots' tomorrow and get a new lot. What is Christmas if we can't have lights and decorations? When we were kids, Christmas was fun. Ear-tingling cold and so white it even made Edmonton shine. We'd wake up at four and dash into Mum and Dad's bedroom. Dad would come downstairs with us while we opened our presents. He'd make a cup of tea and sit watching while we ripped off the wrapping paper, as excited as we were to see if they'd got us what we wanted.

*

"Want a cup of tea, dear?" Mum shouts.

"Yes, please."

I'm in the loft, sorting out the decorations. I'm going for maximum kitsch, just as Dad did when we were kids; paper chains crowding the ceiling, tree bent double under a barrage of baubles and more tinsel and gold lametta than even Liberace could stomach. Mustn't forget the robins. They've got wires round their feet so you can attach them to the tree. Dad sticks them on the Marks and Sparks prints in the living room. They start off upright but by Boxing Day they're leaning off the frames, staring at the carpet.

I get Dad's hammer and set to work. Two hours later I've used every roll of sellotape, nail and pin in the house and have plasters on both thumbs, but I'm happy. Santa Claus is definitely coming to town. I know because we live in his grotto.

Mum walks out to the kitchen carrying the dirty cups. "I don't know why you have to go so mad."

Dad smiles. He does.

## Jack

Makes me livid, having to be helped. I can't even get out of the bath on my own. Stella has to heave me out like a bucket of old rags.

"Shall I do your bits?" she asked this morning.

"You leave my bits alone," I said.

I'm not that far gone. Won't let her sit me on the lavvy, either. She'll be wiping my arse next. I let her help me to the door then tell her I can manage. I can't always. I fell off yesterday. Knocked my head on the corner of the bath and woke up sniffing blue shag pile.

Stella was banging away on the door, shouting, "Are you all right?"

I told her to bugger off.

When I got my strength back, I crawled to the door, reached up and unlocked it. Got a right earful. I'm never to lock the door again. Seventy-eight and I'm treated like a bloody two-year-old. What the hell have things come to?

# Valerie

"Shall I walk down the road with you?" Mum asks next morning, when she sees me in my coat and gloves. I feel like Michelin-woman. I'm wearing a vest, long-sleeve t-shirt, thick jumper, tights and woolly socks under my jeans. Good job Gianni's not here. By the time I got my clothes off, I'd never feel like sex.

"I could do with a bit of fresh air and your Dad's all right," she says. "He never gets up before lunchtime now."

"I'd rather go on my own. Still got a few things to get."

The truth is I've bought five phone cards and I'm off to ring my neighbours. They're keeping an eye on the flat. It's not that I don't trust them. I just need to hear the burglar hasn't returned, that the place is still in one piece. I'd phone every hour if I dared. I don't call from home because I don't want to worry the old folks.

The flat's fine. "Don't worry," my neighbour says. "You needn't bozzer to ring every day."

I will, though. Just in case.

I cross three sets of traffic lights to the other side of the new road and stroll down through the tatty market into what is euphemis-tically called the shopping precinct. Mums in shell suits drag screaming kids past McDonalds, juddering techno noise throbs from the doors of gloomy boutiques, weary queues form at sweet stalls selling Technicolor teeth-rotters. A smoggy gust whips in from the market and whirls up clouds of greasy litter. God, it's dirty, I think, then tell myself not to be a snotty-nosed Swiss. I am though. More Swiss than a fondue fork on my worst days. Sitting on the loo this morning, I made a mental note to wait till Mum's out then clean it properly.

## Jack

"Shall we do the crossword?" Valerie says.

We've done them for years, ever since she was a kid. We've got our routine when she's at home – the Sunday roast, Stella's apple pie then The Times. It's a sort of competition to see who can get the most clues fastest. At least, that's what we did as long as I could write. Since I had that flu, my hands shake so much I have a job with a signature, let alone anything else. I don't want her to see that. Don't want her to think her father's a bloody cripple. When I've had my operation and things are back to normal, I'll start the crosswords again. Get in a bit of practice before she comes home so I'm in with a chance.

"No, dear," I say. "Don't feel like it today."

She chucks the paper in the stand and walks out to the kitchen.

## Valerie

I open my eyes, flick the light switch and squint at my watch. Five o'clock. I try burrowing back under the duvet but it doesn't work. I just get wider and wider awake and start dwelling on why I'm alone for what seems like the millionth Christmas when everyone else is part of a couple. Haven't seen Gianni for a while. He never phoned after I stood him up for the concert and I don't see why I should. And the date with Max was a fiasco.

I'd wafted out to Oberwil, radio full blast, me and Bryan Adams both yelling *Can't Stop This Thing We Started.* I was secretly hoping Max was getting divorced, moving out at the very least. He was sitting at our usual table, looking out across choppy water, familiar smile hovering, eyes warm and flirty.

"A spritzer and I'll have another beer."

He didn't wait to ask what I wanted. He didn't have to. He knows me down to the gusset of my M and S tights. The drinks came and we sat in silence, him lounging, me with elbows on the table, chin resting on my hands. I couldn't keep the broad grin from my face. I was there with him. Together again.

"Pity about the job."

Still smiling, I picked up my glass. "What do you mean?"

The school is divided into three chunks; Lower School, Upper School, Economics and Law. The Head of Upper School had just announced he was retiring early. I'd heard it took him ten minutes to take his tablets every morning and his GP was refusing to prescribe them anymore. I'd thought about it and decided to apply. It would be tough – the present Head put in a twelve-hour day- but it was a challenge and a step up in what had become a dead-end job. I still enjoyed teaching but was bored out of my mind. However many new exercises you do, however many times you change course books, there are only so many ways of teaching modal auxiliaries

"I am sorry," Max said, lighting a cigarette.

What the hell was he talking about?

He drummed his fingers on the table. "Just handed in my application."

I don't know why I was shocked. He'd been at school almost as long as me, was good at his job and highly ambitious, just like me. Of course he'd apply.

"So I take it you'll withdraw yours." Said with the confidence of Cruft's Supreme Champ.

"Why should I?"

He switched to fatherly mode, looked as if he was about to reach across the table and pat me on the back. "Well, I stand more chance of getting the job, obviously."

I reminded myself that Swiss women only got the vote in the seventies. "Things have moved on in case you hadn't noticed. It's not *Kinder, Kirche, Küche* for every woman. Even if that's how you choose to live."

He sighed. "I knew this would be difficult."

"Afraid of the competition?"

He laughed. "Don't be so daft. I'm just thinking of you. Don't want you getting hurt."

"How very kind."

He picked up his cigarettes, waved them in my direction.

I shook my head.

"Look, Val. Anita can't possibly work, not with the twins. I've got to think of the future. How I'm going to pay for their education and all that."

How dare he mention the reality I didn't want to hear? I took a slug of my drink and nicked one of his cigarettes. "I'm divorced, got no private means. Who do you think is going to provide for me? Anyway, I need a challenge." I narrowed my eyes and glared at him through the smoke. "Need to move on. Not that I ever wanted to."

He frowned and looked out across the lake. A cormorant was standing on a horizontal branch that dipped into the water, dissecting a fish. "You've always said you hated admin." He stubbed out his cigarette. "There'd be an awful lot of that."

"It comes with the territory. There are compensations."

"Thinking of the increased status, are we?"

"And you're not?"

He picked up the empty cigarette packet and crumpled it. "I don't want you to suffer like Harald. Just look at the state he's in. Do you want to age overnight? Think of the hours. You'd have no private life to speak of."

"You're the one with the family."

"I've talked it over with Anita. She'll support me whatever I do."

Hail to the Subservient Swiss Wife, I thought, the green-eyed monster roaring in my ears.

"The point is I'm not sure you'd be able to cope. And don't think I'm saying that to get at you, but you're easily upset and you often take things personally. Behave like that and you'll be in a padded cell before you know it."

"I am quite capable of drawing the line between work and play." Not quite true; after his wedding I'd avoided the staffroom for months. But I'd matured since then, and in any case I had every intention of winning.

His eyes took on a metallic gleam. "Be a shame, though. I really don't want to fight, Val."

"Me, neither."

We finished our drinks in a silence so sharp you could have slit throats on it. He didn't offer to pay. I wouldn't have let him. As we got up to go, the cormorant took a last peck at the bones, picked up the skeleton and tossed it into the lake.

I shrug off his memory with the duvet and get up. Best to be busy on a day like this. Best not to think of Daddy Max doling out presents to another woman's children.

Eight o' clock. I've showered, washed my hair, slapped on a ton of make-up and I'm starving. Had breakfast at six and the smell of bacon basting the turkey is driving me mad. I've already nicked two rashers. Think I'll have a couple of sour cream and onion Pringles, just to tide me over. Or maybe a handful. Not much point in leaving those three in the tin. There's too much stuff in that drinks cupboard anyway.

Twelve o' clock. I can hear Mum upstairs, getting HRH ready for the Royal Progress down to the plebs. It takes him half an hour hanging onto Mum and the banisters as tight as he can. He shuffles in, a pale phantom in a terry-towelling dressing gown and lambswool slippers. I'll just pour myself a drink to keep the smile on my face.

"Morning." He lets go of Mum's arm and sags into the old green armchair he's sat in since the year dot. "Happy Christmas."

I bend down and kiss his bony cheek. "Happy Christmas, Dad."

"What'll you have for breakfast?" Mum asks.

Daft question. He always has two Shredded Wheat. Mountains could crumble, oceans run dry, volcanoes spew megatonnes of lava onto every single shore but in Ponders End you'd still hear my Dad chomping on two Shredded Wheat.

"I'll just have a slice of toast, dear," he says. "Not very hungry today."

That puts me off my stride so much I have to get myself a gin and tonic to steady my nerves.

Two o' clock. I'm chasing a sprout round my plate, wondering why I can never get Dad anything he wants. Paul and Mum liked their presents, with Dad it was the same farce as every year. I know I always get him a jumper but that's only because he's so difficult. I spent ages looking for this one. Cost a packet, too.

He doesn't want books. "I get them from the library."

He doesn't like Swiss chocolates. "Too rich for me."

He doesn't listen to music. "I like James Last."

Well stuff it, Dad, there are limits.

So I slogged round every menswear shop in the western hemisphere and how did he react? Held it up in front of him like something he'd fished out of a sewer and said, "I've never had a brown one before."

I want a real Christmas. One like on the telly with a table of happy people stuffing their faces, pulling crackers and chattering nineteen to the dozen. All you can hear at ours is the scraping of steel on china and the occasional belch from Dad. He's finished now, licked his fork and put it next to his knife, right in the centre of his plate, not one degree left or right. Any second now he'll start the torture. I pour myself another glass of bubbly, hoping it'll make me deaf.

Thwack, thwack, thwack. He's cleaning his dentures. There's a gap between his plate and his teeth and he nuzzles the food out with his tongue then sucks it down his gullet like a drain. The more you try not to listen the more you do.

"More champagne, Dad, Mum?" Paul doesn't drink so there's no point in asking him.

I finish it off. With any luck I'll drop off and wake up somewhere else.

Five o'clock. I wake up in hell, opening gritty eyes. Very slowly.

"Fancy a drink and a sandwich?" Mum says.

Hair of the dog? Why not?

Dad creeps to the table on Paul's arm and collapses in front of a plate of *nouvelle cuisine*. A quarter of a ham sandwich, all the crusts cut off, a tiny pile of shiny brown pickle and half a tomato.

"Tha' all you havin'?" I seem to be having difficulty with my speech. Better keep my big gob shut.

"Yes," he says. "But I will have a pickled walnut."

I don't know why I don't help him. I sit, preserved in booze, watching him try to stab a walnut onto his fork. Once, twice, three times. Each time he misses. Each time the fork gets farther away from the jar.

And then I do the unforgivable. I laugh. It's not a real laugh, more a schoolkid's snigger. He looks down at his red and gold paper serviette. Feeling guilty as hell, I prod two walnuts onto the end of my fork and put them on his plate. "'Ere y'are."

Two wrinkled brown balls. Two pickled aneurisms.

Seven o' clock. Mum comes down from putting Dad to bed. "Who's for a piece of Christmas cake and a drink?"

Half an hour later we're splitting our sides over Trivial Pursuit.

"Noggin the Nog," Paul says and we scream with laughter as if it's the Joke of the Year.

Can't play it when Dad's around. He swears at Mum and upsets her. It's a laugh, though, the three of us. No-one's taking it seriously. Can't do that with Dad. He takes everything seriously. I remember Mum talking about their sex life once, not that I wanted to hear. "He never laughs," she said. "It's always a performance." A performance of what?

During a port and marzipan lull we hear a noise. Soft, insistent tapping from above. Like a very polite death-watch beetle.

"Whassat?"

"I'll go and see," Paul offers.

I stagger to my feet. "No, 'ssallright. You've to do it allatime. I go."

The stairs sway a bit but I totter gamely into Dad's bedroom.

He's half hanging out of bed, hitting at the floor with an old wooden backscratcher.

"Waddayawant, Dad?"

He looks up, tears filling pale eyes. "Don't leave me alone up here in the dark."

I slink downstairs and we pack up the game. Paul goes and sits with him till he falls asleep. Mum and I empty a bottle of gin and crunch our way through a family bag of Cheese and Onion, staring into space, avoiding each other's eyes.

\*

Sitting at the Park Hotel bar in *Industriestrasse,* Zug, vodka and tonic in hand, I look up and catch the smile of an Armani-suited fifty-something. He raises his glass, we exchange muted 'cheers' and two cashews later he's buying me the fourth vodka of my post-England aperitif. I've dumped my case at the station. Can't face the thought of walking into a dark, empty flat with the last ten days' bills for company.

It turns out he's Viennese, which I like, owns a chain of dry-cleaner's, which I don't, but the vodka says you can't have every-thing. He's in town for a dry-cleaner's convention. I don't listen to a word of what he's saying; just concentrate on his wonderful accent. I love the way the Viennese roll their vowels, smooth the harshness out of German, turn *Eisbein* into *Sachertorte.*

Three more vodkas later we take the lift up to his room. As he unlocks the door, the sub-zero temperature makes me gasp. All the windows are wide open.

"A thousand pardons, *Süsses,*" he says, seeing me clutch my jacket to my throat. "I hate stuffy hotel rooms, don't you?"

The thought of leaving flicks through my mind but I discard it with my tights. I know what I've come for even if goose pimples are breaking out on my legs.

He closes the windows, smile as silky as the duvet cover. "Music?"

"No."

I walk over to him and kiss him on the mouth. His lips are damp, slightly slobbery. I pull away and start to unbutton his belt. He takes my hand and lifts it to his lips.

"What's the hurry? We have all night, don't we? Or is there a husband waiting at home?"

I shake my head and return to undoing his belt, open his flies with a swift 'zip' and reach for the necessary.

I dress as quickly as I can.

"I'll be here all weekend. May I telephone you?"

"I don't think so."

At the station the left-luggage office is empty. It takes fifteen minutes of bell pressing to summon an attendant who chucks my case at me and shuts the glass partition with as much of a thud as he can without smashing it to bits. My flat is cold – the heating's off. Neighbours must have forgotten when I was coming back. I open the fridge. Better make myself a coffee, try and sober up. No milk. Fine. Black's got fewer calories anyway. I reach for the tin next to the expresso machine. No coffee. Could have herbal tea but I'm not that desperate. I pour myself a glass of water, walk out into the hall and turn the thermostat to full blast.

An hour later it's still so cold I make myself some herbal tea to keep the blood from freezing in my veins. I climb into bed fully clothed. I shut my eyes in the hope that I'll fall asleep, but feel myself starting to rotate, faster and faster. The room's doing likewise so I get up and shower, turn the dial from cold to hottest, watch my skin go from milk, through rosé to burgundy. I stand under the water, steam clouds rising around me, until my skin is as shrivelled as the California dates I take Mum at Christmas. Despite the heat I shiver.

# Chapter Five

## January 1996

### Valerie

I squint in my compact mirror, slick an Estée Lauder pout onto my lips, pay the cab driver and march through the hospital gates.

"He's in Bramley Ward," Mum says. "There are three for the elderly. Bramley, Cox and Nelson Mandela. Good job your dad's not in there."

I've read about geriatric wards but this one doesn't fit the cliché. The walls are Caribbean turquoise, the curtains springtime Med dotted with faint yellow stars. Happy kindergarten colours, everything spotlessly clean. The only sign that someone's ill is the screen round the bed opposite Dad's. There are three beds on either side of the ward, each with its own table, locker and plum plastic armchair. Dad's enthroned in the third chair to the left, glaring out of the window.

His feet are in giant slippers, his ankles as swollen as beetroot.

"What's up with his feet?"

"Bad circulation," Mum says. "They've all got it."

It's true. Every single patient has bell-bottom feet. Even the tiniest one, an aged sparrow-woman clambering into bed as if scaling the north face of the Eiger.

"He'll be so pleased to see you," Mum says. "We didn't tell him you were coming. It'll be a lovely surprise."

Sensing someone's talking about him, he turns his head, tuts and looks away.

Mum is undeterred. "Look who's here," she says, planting a kiss on his cheek.

"I can see who it is." He looks at me with angry eyes. "I didn't want you to see me like this."

"Mum said you'd had a stroke."

"We don't really know," Mum says.

How the hell can you not know if someone's had a stroke? "Haven't you talked to the doctors?"

"Don't get stroppy with your mother," Dad says. "I don't want to talk about it."

I scour the ward in search of a safe subject of conversation, trying not to look at Dad's hands. They're clasped in his lap but every now and then they break out and do a little jig. They're covered in red blotches that weren't there at Christmas.

"Nice in here, isn't it?"

He scowls. "It's a dump. Not a patch on Bart's."

Mum and I glance round, hoping none of the staff are within hearing distance.

"But you couldn't go to Bart's, Jack," Mum soothes. "It was an emergency."

"Don't see why not."

"What did you have for lunch?" Maybe a change of topic'll make him more amenable.

There's a pause while he thinks.

"Can't remember," he says finally. "But whatever it was, it was crap."

An Indian elf in saffron shirt and baggy, white trousers approaches, pushing a tea trolley.

"Hallo, Jack," he smiles, eyes shining like polished mahogany. "Ready for your cuppa?"

Dad smiles and nods. "Yes please, Sanjeev."

Contrary old bugger. If he saw Sanjeev outside the hospital, he wouldn't give him the time of day.

"Sugar?"

"Three, please," Dad replies. "It'll cover the taste of the petrol."

Mum and I exchange a glance. Sanjeev doesn't bat an eyelid.

"Would you like one?" Sanjeev asks Mum.

"Yes, please." She ferrets in a Tesco's carrier and takes out two brown paper bags. "I've brought your bananas and your doughnut. Would you like them with your tea?"

"Not my bananas," he decrees with a dismissive wave. "You know I save them for later."

I decide to give it one last try. "They look like nice people in here."

"Who?" he demands, screwing up his eyes and chomping on his doughnut like a donkey.

"I don't know... the patients."

He flicks sugar off his fingers and smacks his lips. "They're clowns."

"You look fine, though. They must be feeding you well."

"Just about edible," he concedes. "But they never give you what you want."

"It's not a good idea to ask him about the food," Mum says on the way out. "Best keep off the subject altogether. They get a menu and have to tick off what they want for the next day."

"What's wrong with that? Sounds like a five-star hotel."

Mum opens the scuffed plastic door that separates Orchard Wing from the leafy affluence of Enfield Ridgeway. "The problem is they can never remember what they've ordered. Almost had a punch-up last Friday. It's always fish, of course, but only one of them had ordered it. It did smell lovely. I quite fancied a bit myself. Well, they all swore blind it was theirs, your Dad loudest of all. But they only had the one helping, for the lady in the bed opposite Arthur's. I thought the others were going to lynch her, they were getting so het up. Your Dad went berserk. Refused to eat a thing if he couldn't have fish and chips." She laughs. "It was funny, really. I didn't dare laugh, though. There would have been hell to pay."

Walking to the car, I slip my arm through hers, squeeze it tight.

"Seeing you'll do him the world of good," she says. "It'll perk him up a treat."

I kiss her cheek, take the car keys out of her hand. "I'll drive. I know you're not really keen."

"You sure, love? Not tired from your flight?"

I close the passenger door after her, swallow a yawn and adjust the driver's seat. "I'm fine."

## Jack

You could see they were itching to go. Well, good riddance. I won't have people coming because they have to. I've got a bit of pride left even if I am in this dump.

Made me mad when Valerie said how nice the place is. She should try being stuck here. They make a bloody great fuss of giving you a menu, saying you've got a choice. Load of drivel. Take the day before yesterday. I'd ordered turkey 'cos I fancied a bit of meat, and what did I get? Pork, if you please. Everybody knows I never eat pork. Never have done, far too fatty. But would they believe it?

I told them what they could do with it, which set them off in a right panic. 'Cos they know damn well if Dr Khan sees I haven't eaten, he'll be down on them like a bucket of that Balti muck my lot are so fond of. He's a coon, of course. Has to be with a name like that. But he's all right. Very polite. "Good morning, Mr Sterling," he always says, "and how are our bowels today?" Talk of the devil. Here he comes now with two housemen, white coat billowing out behind him as if he's on some crusade.

"Good afternoon, Mr Sterling," he says. "I'd like these young chaps to have a look at your aneurisms if you don't mind."

I was planning to settle down with my new Wilbur Smith but I'll help him out. I'm an interesting case, after all, and these young blokes have got to learn.

One of the housemen pulls the screen round my bed and I drop my trousers. The other one has a dekko then moves out of the way for his mate.

"Mr Sterling isn't with us because of the aneurisms," Dr Khan explains. "He probably had a TIA."

"What the hell's that when it's at home?"

"A mini-stroke," he says.

"Didn't feel mini to me. I went all weak and dizzy. Couldn't talk. And what's all this 'probably'? Aren't you sure?"

"We didn't find any major brain damage but we're going to give you a CT scan to make sure."

"When are you operating on the aneurisms?" the first houseman asks.

I get in quick so there's no misunderstanding. "I'm down for Bart's. Mr Macbeth's team."

"Of course we could operate here," Khan says with a smile. "Then your family wouldn't have the inconvenience of trekking up to town to visit."

"They won't mind," I say. "They're happy to come wherever I am."

"You could think about it," Khan says.

His housemen nod sagely.

"Why do you want to keep me here? Are you saying I'm not fit to travel?"

"Not at all," he has to admit. "I'm very pleased with your progress."

"Good." I pick up my book, open it at the page where a patrol of Japs walk straight into an ambush. "Then I'll be out of this place in no time."

## Valerie

"They won't let me smoke," he moans. It's just me and Paul today. We've left Mum at home to rest.

"'Course not, it's a hospital," I snap. This flying over every fortnight is wearing me out. I'm sick of marking in the departure lounge at Kloten and preparing Monday's lessons at Heathrow.

"Here are your bananas and your doughnut, Dad," Paul says. "Mum thought you might like some orange juice."

Dad won't be put off, though. "They all smoke."

I stifle a yawn. "Who does?"

"The staff." He nods towards the nurses' station. "That shower." He gives me a critical once over. "You ought to get to bed earlier. Getting bags under your eyes."

"I've never seen any of the staff smoke," Paul says.

There's a gleam in Dad's eye. "'Course not. They wait till you've gone. Then they come in here and smoke in front of me, to get my goat."

Paul peels a banana and offers it with the same gesture you'd use to pacify an out-of-sorts chimp. "What've you been up to today, then, Dad?"

Dad examines the banana then starts munching. "Been down the gym, as usual."

I nearly laugh out loud. He's never done any sports. Strictly Churchillian, my father.

"I call it the torture chamber," he confides. "I stroll down there every morning, do my exercises, back in time for coffee."

He finishes the banana then offers the skin to me. Paul intercepts it and drops it in the bin next to Dad's bed.

"On my way back today I found a leaflet about smoking," Dad continues. "And it says quite clearly, every patient is allowed six cigarettes a day. No more than that, see, 'cos it wouldn't be healthy."

I glance at Paul, raise my eyes. "Where is this leaflet, Dad? I'd like to have a look at it."

He screws up his eyes. "Don't you believe me?"

"'Course we do." Paul pats Dad's shoulder. "It'd interest me, too, though."

He leans towards us. His breath is heavy, pungent. I wonder if they check that he cleans his teeth. "I had it in my locker but they nicked it."

"Nurse," the old man in the next chair bleats. "Bring me the phone. I've got to make an urgent call." His green and gold tie is spattered with assorted stains, the buttons of his cardigan are done up wrong.

"Poor old sod," Dad says. "Mad as a hatter."

"It's his son," Paul explains. "If he's not here at three on the dot, Charlie thinks he's had an accident."

I glance at my watch. Two minutes past three. We've been here five. Time's handed in his winged chariot. On Bramley Ward he uses a Zimmer frame like the rest of them.

The little sparrow who got Dad's fish and chips is huddled in her bed, blanket drawn up over her head. Dad's eagle eye follows my gaze.

He jabs his chest with his fist, making a hollow sound like banging on plasterboard. "Don't look at her," he shouts. "You're here to visit me!"

"You're allowed to nod at them when you come and go," Paul says, "but nothing more. He's got very possessive."

"And don't keep whispering," Dad spits. "It's very rude."

Half a lifetime later Paul and I wander down to the bus-stop. We have to use public transport as Paul won't drive. It's all part of his New Age philosophy. No harm to the planet and all that crap. I'll hire a car at the airport next time. Dad hasn't got possessive, I think to myself. It's the way he's always been. He didn't want me once I started to voice opinions that differed from his own but he didn't want anyone else to have me, either. Ewan, my sixth-form squeeze was bad enough but the one he really went ballistic over was Dick.

I'd slogged at the chemist's with Mum and Dick every Saturday from pimply third-former to platform-heeled A-Level loutette. At Poly I'd shot up the slave-job ladder to M and S, The Pantheon, Oxford Circus.

"Dick was asking after you," Mum said one Monday I'd spent skipping lectures to fill up shelves with Black Forest gateau. I gave him a ring after Harry Hartley's lecture on *Die Wahlverwandschaften*. A week later on half-day closing we took a boat down the Thames, chatting and looking at the majestic skyline rising out of stewed-tea water.

"Tell me about college."

I made it sound better than it was – a gloomy, dust-infested dump for both kinds of D-Grade students: those of minimal intelligence and those who had screwed up their A-Levels by screwing instead of revising.

I'd always liked Dick. I liked his freckles and the way his hair curled into the nape of his neck. By the time we got off the boat at Hampton Court, he was holding my hand. We got lost in the maze, started to snog then took a taxi back to the flat-cum-slum I was renting with three Lindas and a Celia.

"He's old enough to be your Dad," Mum grumbled. "And you can't love him because of the way his hair curls."

It wasn't just that. He was interested in me and that was irresistible. He'd ask what I was reading then ring Grant and Cutler's and order the books, too. How could I not love a bloke who'd do battle with the *Nibelungen* or wade through *Der Grüne Heinrich* on my account? I told Harry Hartley I wasn't doing my year abroad. Nine months away from Dick, buried in a corner of Bavaria? He might forget me, might not want me when I came back. I wasn't that stupid.

In the summer we went to Brighton. He said I was wonderful, a great lover, much better than his wife. When he got home, there was a letter waiting for him. Someone had told her about us. So she wrote to him, saying she loved him but that he'd have to give me up.

She wrote to him. He wrote to me. I went to bed for a week.

"All men are bastards," Linda 1 said, stuffing a Benson's into my mouth.

Celia, who was a dab hand at sewing Harrods' labels into her home-made gear, gave me a genteel hug. "We're going to a party at

Geoff's on Saturday. There'll be masses of men there. I'll run you up a pair of hot pants if you like."

I'd spent my rent money on clothes and booze consolation so had to move home, which would have been all right had Dick not picked me up one day after Poly. I went back to lying, reasoning that it was all my parents' fault. They couldn't take the truth, so I lied. Things were fine until my birthday, when I met Dick for a quick fumble on the Piccadilly Line. He gave me an LP – *Cosi fan Tutte.* When I showed it to Mum and Dad, saying I'd got it from Celia, I forgot that I'd stuffed his birthday card down the sleeve.

"Your father's going mad," Mum said. "He wants you out of here tomorrow."

I wanted to grab him by the throat, yell that Mum had told me about his affairs when I caught her crying into the washing-up one night. What was so different about mine? I didn't. There was no point. I just packed a bag and moved out. Celia said she'd lend me next month's rent money. I didn't go home for a while.

Paul puts his arm round my shoulder and I bury my head in his donkey jacket, inhaling a warm mix of wool, Body Shop soap and marihuana. I wonder if they ever told him why I'd disappeared. Probably not.

"Here's the bus to the town," he says. "Might have to wait for a connection when we get to Enfield. Could go for a coffee?"

I stand on tiptoe, kiss his cheek. "I want to do some shopping anyway. Need your advice."


## Jack

Nobody came to see me this afternoon. It often happens. Stella says someone turns up every day but she's lying. She's not doing it to be contrary but I know what I'm talking about. I have a little nap and when I wake up, that Jasmine's peering into my face.

"You want to watch that," I say. "Almost gave me a fright." Her big black gob so close to mine.

She puts a kidney dish with a syringe and four small glass phials onto my bedside cupboard. "Wanted to make sure you were all right, didn't I?" she says. "You were talking to yourself again."

I don't like her use of the word 'again'. What's the silly cow implying? "What was I talking about?"

"Sounded like some kind of battle. Were you in the War, Jack? All those books on your locker. Never seen you read anything else."

"'Course I was. Think I was a deserter, do you, or a conchie?"

She looks blank.

"Conscientious objector," I explain. "Don't they teach you anything at school these days?"

"I'd like to hear about it, from someone who was there." She makes it sound as if it was the Battle of bloody Agincourt.

"Well, ask Arthur. He'll tell you what you want to hear."

The truth's nothing for a woman's ears. And anyway, she doesn't really want to know. She's just being nosy like the rest of them.

"Got to take some blood," she says, picking up the syringe. She takes hold of my arm and swabs a bit. "You've got nice veins, Jack."

That makes me laugh. "That's the first time a woman's complimented me on that part of my anatomy."

She gives my cheek a crafty stroke before I can turn away. "Bet you're a right one with the ladies."

"I had my moments."

Got nice hands, that Jasmine. Dainty fingers. No rings, I notice. "You courting?"

"Why? Gonna make me an offer?" She's sneaked the needle into my arm and the first phial's filling up. "Your daughter and son married?"

"My daughter was." I wish I could still say she is.

Jasmine takes the phial off the needle, replaces it with the next one. "You've got very good-looking children. Take after your wife's side, do they?"

She chuckles, cheeky cow. "Always wanted to get married, me," she says, before I have time to reply, "wear a long white dress. Bet your daughter looked good in hers."

"She did," I say. "She looked a picture."

A damn sight better than a great fat lump like you, I think to myself.

"Bet you were proud." She eases the needle out of my arm. "Put your finger on the vein for me so I can undo a plaster."

"'Course I was." I want to tell her to bugger off and mind her own business but I don't. The thought of Valerie in her wedding dress makes my eyes go all musty. Just like they did on the day. She looked so beautiful, like one of those Greek goddesses, all calm and serene.

I wasn't too sure about KM the first time we met. Bit of a stuffed shirt, I thought, that Saturday afternoon when she brought him home. Stella was in the kitchen, giving the floor a going-over; I was in the living room, having my weekly turf-out of the papers. He was smartly turned-out but overdressed for a weekend in a suit and tie. I felt a right bloody fool in my working bags. He shook my hand, did a little bow and said, "Good afternoon, sir." Very formal, these Swiss, I thought to myself, but a pleasant change from the clowns she'd been with before.

Stella asked if he'd like tea or coffee and he said he'd rather have coffee if it was no trouble.

"We've only got instant. I'm afraid," she said.

He said that would be fine, he often drank it himself.

"You do it," she said to Valerie. "You know how he likes it. What are you having, Jack?"

I don't know why she asked. I only drink coffee of a morning. The women disappeared into the kitchen so I told him to take a pew. I put the papers in the corner by the stand so I wouldn't forget to chuck them, then sat down and flicked the dust off my trousers.

"And how do you like London?"

I'd heard via Stella that he'd been sent over by his firm to learn the language. It was one of those Swiss insurance companies, offices all over the world. Valerie'd got a job there after college.

"Great," he said. "It's a brilliant city, so much bigger than Zurich. It took me a while to find my way around." He smiled. "Soon found White Hart Lane, though."

"Did you, now?"

"I live in Zurich," he said, "so I'm a Grasshoppers supporter, but I've always followed Spurs."

The girls came in with the tea-tray.

"This young fellow's been telling me he supports that other lot."

Valerie raised her eyes and gave him a bit of a look. "Dad's an Arsenal man."

The cup rattled in the saucer as she put my tea on the table. "He has got a name, Dad. It's Klaus-Maria."

Bloody hell, I thought. He won't last long in the Temple Bar. "Am I right in thinking Maria's the same as Mary?"

"Yes." He put his coffee cup down on the table. "My parents were living in Bavaria when I was born. It's a common name there."

"Well, it isn't round here." I was concerned for the poor bugger. "Haven't you got a second name we could call you by?"

"No," he said, cool as a Fox's Glacier. "My parents thought Klaus-Maria was enough."

"Well, there's nothing else for it, lad," I said. "You'll have to be KM."

"All right, sir," he said, and carried on sipping his coffee right as ninepence.

Valerie wasn't touching hers. She was sitting there, glaring at me as if I was the bloody Devil.

Stella picked up the cake slice. "Would anyone like some Battenberg, Jack's favourite?"

"No, thanks, Mum." Valerie got up and dragged the poor sod to his feet.

"Let the lad finish his coffee," I said. "No need to rush off."

But she wasn't having any of it. She shot him out of the house before I'd had a chance to talk to him.

"Bloody rude," I said to Stella when they'd gone. "What will the lad think of us?"

Stella said I'd upset Valerie, but that was nothing to how riled I got over that letter from his parents. Valerie wanted to get married in London. Sensible, her mother and I thought. They'd have to live in Zurich, what with KM not being able to extend his work permit. He'd have stayed here otherwise, I know that for a fact. So Stella worked out what we could afford and wrote to KM's parents inviting them to the church and reception. I remember every bloody word that father of his wrote back.

*Dear Sir and Madam*, it started,

*I am writing to inform you that we will not visit the wedding of your daughter with our son. These are the reasons: We only met your daughter at one occasion. Unfortunately she is not at all that what we wish in a daughter-in-law. As my wife says, she has an alien faith, none of the abilities of a good housewife and dresses in a manner which would endanger Klaus-Maria's career prospects, which are very big indeed.*

*By the speed with which the betrothal took place we are concluding that you employed some trick to make our son marry a woman who can never give him satisfaction. It would be better if the young people would separate themselves for a time to find out what their true feelings are.*

*If Klaus-Maria goes ahead, we will cut off his inheritance, which, we are suspecting, is the object you and your daughter are bent to obtain.*

*Yours sincerely*
*Margrit and Rudolf H. Bumbacher.*

I wasn't going to show it to Stella but she kept nagging so in the end I did. Didn't show her or Valerie the letter I wrote back, though. Not on your nelly.

We met them on our first trip to Switzerland. They invited the four of us for Sunday lunch. What could I say? Couldn't upset the poor little bugger again, not after what his own family'd done. His mother was all right, not a bad-looking woman, but that father of his was a matchbox tyrant if ever I saw one. You often find that with shortarses. The blokes, I mean. Try to make up for looking like bugger all, even when they're dressed up. Not that he was wearing anything half-way decent. I put on better togs to mow the bloody lawn.

## Valerie

Oh, happy day! It's Sunday and I can go home tonight. Back to a world that doesn't stink of Dettol, floor polish and sundry bodily fluids.

The screen round Charlie's bed is drawn today. Dad's leaning over one side of his chair, trying to peer through the gap at one of the corners.

He hears us approach and turns round. "Have you got my bananas?"

"Yes, dear."

"Why don't you bring a bunch?" I wonder.

"They'd go black," Mum says, taking off her coat. "It's that hot in here."

Dad shivers. "Freezing, isn't it? They've left the heating off again."

He takes his doughnut out of the bag, gives it a quick once-over then plops it back. "Is it homemade?"

"I've never made doughnuts," Mum says with a laugh. "You know that."

"It's very easy," he explains. "I don't know what you make such a fuss about. All you do is slosh things into a bowl, mix them up and Bob's your uncle."

Masterchef, whose culinary skills stretch to boiling an egg.

"What's this?" he says, as I hand him a square shape wrapped in dark blue paper. "Doesn't look like my chocolate biscuits."

"Open it and see. Thought I'd get you something useful."

"You shouldn't spend all this money on me," he grumbles, ripping off the paper as fast as Paul and I used to on Christmas morning. He opens the box, removes the white Styrofoam and holds up the latest Nokia mobile. Sleek black plastic, state-of-the-art, cost me a fortune.

"What's this, then?"

"You can see what it is, Jack," Mum smiles. She pats my knee. "Very thoughtful of you, dear."

"I thought it'd be good for you to have, Dad. I can give you a buzz, see how you are. You won't have to bother the nurses."

I'm not suggesting he phone me. I'm not in cloud cuckoo-land yet.

Dad holds the mobile up to the light, turns it upside down, then back upright again. "How do you work it?"

I've done my homework, programmed Mum's, Paul's and my number, so I show him how to call up the directory. Then I get him to select Paul's number. Once, twice, three times, like the teacher I am. When Paul answers, Dad beams like a kid with a new toy. "Hallo, son. You'll never guess what your sister's gone and done."

Dad chats, Mum fusses with his bedside locker and I sit smiling, gobsmacked that for once I might possibly have got him something he likes.

When he stops talking, I show him how to switch the phone off. I want to put it back in its box but he clutches it to his chest.

"They'll nick it as soon as my back's turned," he says. "I might let that Jasmine have a go, though."


## Jack

I watch them walk off the ward and wonder, not for the first time, why my Valerie still hasn't found herself a man. Good-looking girl like her. Paul's on his own, but then he's always been shy. Shame he doesn't take after his old man as far as that's concerned. It'd ease my mind if my kids were settled. Valerie was once. Christ knows why she left. Just wrote to us, saying she was moving out. I put her mother on the blower straight away, asking what the hell was going on but she wouldn't say. Mind you, I'd rather see her on her own than with some of the cretins she had. One in particular; that bloody swine she and Stella used to work for at Cross and Herbert's. Father of four, Catholic, of course – but you could tell his type half a mile off. I bet he'd had more women than the Fifth Army had VD.

I was driving home from town one evening. I'd had a good day, got orders for shirts and ties from all the swanky stores, when all of a sudden a car came towards me and I saw Valerie in the passenger seat. And who was sitting next to her but Dick Fredericks, the little toad. Couldn't do a u-turn, which was a bloody good job for him. I'd have hammered him into the ground soon as look at him, but I tackled Stella as soon as I got home.

Valerie said she was going down to Brighton for a week with one of her mates from college. I didn't say a dicky-bird, just let her go. Then I phoned the bastard's wife. Nice woman. I'd met her a few times when I'd picked Stella up from work and his wife had brought something to the shop. I said he'd asked about some seconds we were selling off cheap. I could drop them round that day. She said he wasn't at home. There was a Pharmaceutical Society conference and he wouldn't be back till the weekend. So I popped in and had a chat with her instead.

Another thing that upset me was not going to Valerie's graduation. I'd been looking forward to it, seeing her walk across the stage in gown and mortar board, first member of the family ever to get that far. She phoned and told Stella she wasn't going, made some excuse. I said to Stella, I bet she went and I bet it was with that toe-rag. And another thing I'd like to know while we're on the subject; did Dickhead try it on with my wife as well as my daughter?

## Valerie

Back in the land of tick-tock efficiency at the end of a perfect school day. Everyone was punctual, had done their homework and seemed to want to learn. Teaching couldn't be better. I'm off to the school play tonight. Have to turn up at all school functions now, especially as Max is parading his three Barbies at every opportunity; school concert, end of term party, the opening of the new fridge in the canteen.

I don't give a shit about him anymore. Partly because I've been reading some shake-yourself-sane manuals, partly because I've got back with Gianni. I know I'm breaking my rule on replays and repeats but he phoned first. And having to learn new names all the time, not to mention get used to each bloke's weird habits was driving me barmy. Got to tidy up my private life, anyway, as headmistress-in-waiting.

I know Max'll be at the play, so I take a couple of hours making up and deciding what to wear – conservative enough for the school governors but sexy enough to let Max the Maggot see what he's missing. I walk into the school hall, see the Heads and governors lined up in the front row so march down and conform to the Swiss custom of shaking hands with everything including the kitchen sink. I sit next to Frau Willimann, wife of the education secretary, and am feigning interest in the smallest of local talk, when a raven-haired Mini-Max plonks herself down beside me. I look up and see Max, Anita and Mini-Max Two approaching. Max gives me a long, pursed-lip look as if to say why can't I sit at the back like all the other lepers. Anita gives a curt nod.

"Come and sit next to me, Mummy," Mini-Max One simpers.

Anita doesn't have the stomach for that so she makes the other kid sit next to her sister then drags Max off to the second row. When the lights go down, Max comes over to check the kids are all right.

"Sit on the chair properly, Angelica," he says to the one next to me. "Have you got a handkerchief? I don't want you sniffing, giving people cause to complain."

Out of the corner of my eye I see him fidget with the child, feel in her pockets for tissues and if we weren't at war and didn't hate each other's guts, I'd swear it's his hand that brushes against my thigh. Don't ask me what the play's about. My mind's gone wonky. It might be one of those gloomy German Naturalist things where everyone is poor and starving at the start and dead at the end.

*

I drag myself home from school the following night, put the kettle on, open a greaseproof bag of *Quarkini* (small doughnuts filled with cream cheese and sultanas) and flop onto the sofa. The phone rings and I consider not answering. Don't feel like talking today, but it might be Gianni. He's coming round tonight to do home-made lasagne and *tiramisu*. Perhaps he wants me to waddle down to the shops for some parmesan.

"Hallo dear."

"Dad?"

I can't remember the last time he phoned. What the hell's happened? Has Mum died?

"Thought I'd see if this thing really does work abroad."

I calm down and take a sip of tea.

"Are you still there?"

"Yes, Dad." You've given me a heart attack but I'm still here, pinching myself that I'm not dreaming.

"I'd like you to have a word with your brother. I'm a bit worried about him."

Why was I daft enough to think he was phoning for me? "He's told you about chucking his job, then?"

"He's started working for this charity place."

"I know. Good, isn't it?" I pick up doughnut number one, get ready to take a bite.

"But he's only a volunteer. He doesn't get paid."

"Sorts the wheat from the chaff. Shows who's really interested."

"But where's it going to get him? It's not a proper job, is it?"

"Dunno, Dad." I knock the doughnut on the side of the plate, get rid of the excess sugar. "You'd better ask him, not me."

There's a pause. "You know what kind of people are in that place, don't you?"

"Yes." Here we go. I take the biggest bite I can manage while still able to speak.

"Bloody drug addicts."

"Ex-addicts, Dad." I spit sugar onto the coffee table, wipe it off with a sleeve. "They're trying to come off it." Well done them. I don't know how I'd react if someone told me I could never have another drink.

There's a half-doughnut pause. "He might end up like them."

"So anyone who works in a psychiatric hospital, assuming there are any that escaped Martinet Thatcher's attention, ends up mad?"

He tuts. "No, of course not."

"Anyone who works with Aids patients catches it?"

He sucks in a whoosh of air. "You never know."

I squeeze doughnut number two, probing for the gooey bit. "Look Dad, from what Paul's told me about the state of those people when they turn up, I think it's more likely to put him off hard drugs forever. All right?"

"You reckon?"

"Yes, Dad."

"You're not just saying that?"

"No, Dad."

"Right," he says, his old self again. "I'd better go, love. It's a bit on the parky side out here. Jasmine says I mustn't catch cold. Risk not having my operation."

"Where are you?"

"In the potting shed."

What's this? Occupational therapy? "What are you doing there?"

It can't be gardening. He pulls out the plants and waters the weeds.

"I'm not allowed to use this phone thing on the ward. Have to come out here."

I hear a deep, mulchy voice. "And have a crafty ciggie. Go on, Jack, admit it."

Just what kind of carer is she? Worried about him catching a cold but she lets him smoke? An old man, arteries about to burst. Is this how she copes with the NHS crisis? Bump them off and free a bed?

"I'll have to go now. Jasmine wants to get back to the ward. You all right, dear?"

"Well, I...." I'd like to tell him about Max but he wouldn't understand. And I don't want that woman blabbing my business all round the nurses' station. "Yes, Dad."

"You're always all right, aren't you?"

"Yes, Dad."

I down doughnut two in three bites, doughnut three in two, pick up the plate and lick off the surplus sugar.

# Chapter Six

## February 1996

### Jack

Charlie's at it again, calling for his wife.

"Meg," he goes. "help me. Save me, please."

I tell her to hurry up about it but it makes no difference. He can keep it up for hours.

Hated him the moment I set eyes on him, walking in here like a bloody sergeant-major. It was one of his lucid moments, no doubt, and he was determined to make the most of it. I don't blame him for that. You've got to. You never know if it's going to be your last.

He strutted up to me and stuck a fat, hairy paw up my nose. "Good morning to you," he said. "Charles is the name."

"Well, you'll be Charlie round here," I muttered, "once they stick a catheter up your arse."

He patted his head, making sure the hair he'd whiplashed from left to right was still in place.

He nodded at the book on my locker: *Even Lions Falter.* "I see you like to remember the old days." He patted the gravy-stained rag poking out of the top of his blazer. "Regimental tie."

I picked up the Mail, hoping it'd put him off.

"Weren't you on active service?" His voice boomed across the ward. Even Arthur and Grandad looked up.

"'Course I was," I hissed. "We all were. Nothing to brag about."

"Best years of my life, the army," he said. "Everyone pulling together. Especially D-Day. There, too, were you?"

I shouldn't have answered. Don't know why I did. Must have been my mouth going AWOL. "I was in Italy."

"Ah," he said. "D-Day dodger. Well, we can't all be where it counts."

Typical, I thought, to quote that Astor woman; a filthy-rich Yank who'd never been near a battlefield in her life. "What D-Day is it you're talking about?" I said. "Salerno, Sicily, Anzio?"

I turned away and shut my eyes. Couldn't bear to look at the pompous git in case I belted him one. Not that he wouldn't have deserved it but it would've been me that got into trouble. Just like all those years ago.

Jasmine's just finished seeing to him now. Coming over for a chat, looks like. He peed his pants again. I'm not criticising him for that, daft bugger. We all do it. There's something about this place that interferes with your water works. But Charlie makes such a damn great fuss about it. Bawls his head off as if it's the end of the world. You lose all your dignity when you come in here. I've told him. Some days it's easier to accept than others.

She's quizzing me again, Jasmine, wanting to know about the War.

"Don't know why you keep on about it," I say. "It's all dead and buried."

She fiddles with the blankets at the bottom of my bed, lifting them out then tucking them in tighter. I have three now. Feel the cold something rotten.

"You could help me for a change," she grins.

"Can't see how."

"I'm doing a project," she says, lowering her voice, "History O-Level. Gonna get my exams. Be a proper nurse."

You'll have your work cut out, I think to myself. You're nowhere near as bright as my Valerie.

She must be reading my mind because she pulls the blankets so hard I think she's going to flatten me. "Just 'cos I do this crappy job doesn't mean I'm thick."

"Don't you get uppity with me, my girl," I say. "I never said anything about you being stupid."

"You gotta be determined. It isn't easy sitting down and studying when you could be watching Eastenders. Not that you'd know anything about night school. Bet you had a good education. You got posh boy stamped all over your forehead."

I laugh out loud at that.

"What are you laughing at?" she says.

"I'm not laughing at you. I take my hat off to anyone who betters themselves. I'm laughing at the life you reckon I've led. Probably had less schooling than you."

She frowns and leans on the iron rail at the foot of my bed. "Can't have less than at comprehensive in Tottenham. Bet you went to grammar school."

"I did get into Leith Academy."

"Ha," she says, "a posh git. I knew it."

"It was a good school. But my parents had no money. I won a scholarship."

"So what?" She looks at me as if I'm Prince Philip bleating about giving up one of the Rolls.

"We moved just before the school year started. My father was transferred to London."

"Must've had a good job," she says, filling a plastic beaker with water. Don't know why she bothers. I only drink my Lemon Barley.

"He was a clerk in Customs and Excise," I say. "Nothing grand, even if he did make out he was First Lord of the Treasury. But London meant more money so we went. When we got to Wood Green, I was bunged straight into Secondary Modern."

"Could have done the exam again, couldn't you?"

"There was never any mention of it."

"What about your old man? He could have gone down the Council, given them a bit of stick."

"Parents didn't protest in those days. Not our sort, anyway." Not that mine would have.

She pats my legs. "So, you gonna tell me, Jack? It'd make all the difference if I could, like, get quotes from someone who was there."

"Must be someone in your own family you could ask."

She frowns and shakes her head. "Only one who'd know's my Gran and she's dead."

"Dad'd be too young, I suppose?"

"Dunno. Mum's never said."

"Died, did he?"

"No. Look, are you gonna help me or not?"

Poor cow, I think, growing up without a father. Must be terrible.

"If I had a bit of peace and quiet. If Arthur was back next to me...," I nod in Charlie's direction, "and he was down the end where he belongs."

She grins. "That's Beverly's job. And she wants him next to you. Says the two noisy ones should be together. Charlie'll be fine if you talk to him nicely."

She messes around with my blankets again and lumbers off. I'm not talking to that bloody goon nicely, I think. Not when he reminds me of someone I hated. And if you're not careful, young lady, I won't be talking to you.


Clive Onions, his name was. Sergeant and Grand Master of Chickenshit. Like Charlie he'd slicked his hair over his skull to hide a bald patch. Had the same voice, too – twice the size of their bodies. Charlie's clean-shaven but Onions had one of those pencil-thin moustaches that made you think he was too bloody mean to grow a proper one.

On his first day he gave us a pep talk.

"I want you men to be on the lookout," he said, moustache quivering like a ferret on heat, "for nuns falling from the sky."

"Do what, Sarge?" I knew I should keep my trap shut but I couldn't.

104

He asked my name.

"Well, Sterling," he said, "I have it on the best authority that German paratroopers disguised as nuns will be dropped near London very soon. That's how they plan to invade, see?"

I laughed out loud; the idea was so bloody preposterous. Soon all the men were laughing with me. That got his goat. "I don't like you, Sterling," he snapped. "You're the slack type. The sort that undermines morale."

He gave me most of the crap jobs after that but I didn't let him get to me. I wasn't going to give him the satisfaction.

Things got worse one night when Bert and I went out on the piss at the only pub in the village. The barmaid was a sweet little thing – all doe eyes and come-hither looks – and as the evening wore on, I ditched Bert and we got chatting. One thing led to another and soon after closing time she and I were horizontal on the snug carpet, being careful not to wake her father.

"You're in for it now," Bert said, next morning. "She's Onions' bint, ain't she?"

From then on I didn't get most of the crap, I got it all. I spent my days scrubbing lavvies, cleaning barracks floors with razor blades or sweeping the parade ground with a toothbrush. But I didn't care. I stowed my feelings away like spare socks in my valise. I knew I was getting to him and that made me the winner.

One Sunday evening after Onions'd come back from leave, he pranced into the kitchen, swank stick stuffed under his arm. Bert used to say he'd had it welded there. I took no notice, carried on gouging eyes out of a King Edward.

"Had a very interesting leave," he said.

"Meet any bearded nuns, did you, Sarge?"

I heard a sharp intake of breath but didn't look up.

"Met some blokes who remember your sister at Sandhurst. They say she was a very popular girl."

I looked at the knife in my hand and told him to leave my sister out of it.

He turned on his heel and marched off. I knew the bastard was grinning.

Next night I was on sentry duty with Bert. I was on more or less permanent night watch by then. Onions thought it would stop me knocking off his bird, which it didn't. Bert had gone for a crap and suddenly Onions popped out from nowhere, a sneer on his greasy face.

"Those blokes I met on leave," he said, "said your sister was such a favourite with the lads they sent her to Africa to cheer up the troops."

"I told you to leave her out of this," I said. "She's got nothing to do with you and me."

"Maybe," he said, twiddling his moustache, "but Rosie has." Rosie was the barmaid. "I've dealt with her, though. She won't be carousing with the likes of you again."

"What have you done to her?" I imagined him slapping her about, knowing she was too naïve, too soft to fight back.

I walked over to him and bent down so I was looking straight into those shifty eyes. "I asked you a question."

"Taught her a lesson," he said. "Given her a bit of the discipline you so blatantly lack."

In the split second before I hit him I knew I'd cop it. He had all the force of the Army behind him, but I didn't give a shit. I grabbed him by the collar so he couldn't duck and punched him right in the middle of his filthy great gob.

"This is for Rosie."

He had no guard up, so I whacked him again.

"And this is for my sister."

He put up his fists but he had no chance. I hit him until he was flat in the dirt, where he belonged. Then I got on top of him and hit him some more. Bert reappeared – I can't remember when – and dragged me off. If he hadn't, I would have killed the bastard.

# Valerie

Max flings open the staffroom door in his usual Monday afternoon temper, clocks the stranger sitting at the coffee table flicking
through last Sunday's Times and, being a well-trained Swiss, strides
up to Gianni, hand outstretched.

"Max Fuchs. Here on teaching practice, are you? One of Val's
students?"

Gianni stands, shakes the proffered hand. "Not exactly."

"Max," I smile, "this is Gianni. Gianni, Max."

Max clears his throat. "Ah, well. Pleased to meet you. Have to
dash, I'm afraid. Got a very important meeting."

Gianni nods, I look blank.

"I've decided to get into politics," Max beams. "Do my bit. Major
party, of course."

"You?" I frown, "in a political party?"

The grin spreads across his face like melting cheese. "Whyever
not?"

"Used to say it bored you to tears."

"Well," he says, "things change. People move on."

I move closer to Gianni, put my arm round his waist.

"As a matter of fact," Max says, "a few town bigwigs have been
wanting me to sign up for quite some time. Might come in handy,
you never know." He smiles at me, nods at Gianni, picks up his
briefcase and sweeps out of the room.

\*

"I don't know what you're worried about, *cara*," Gianni says, after
a performance on my part light years short of the *linguine al limone*
he rustled up for supper.

"If every school governor's a member of a political party and Max
is in the same one, he'll get the rotten job."

"Are they all in the same party?"

"How the hell should I know?" Shouldn't think so, though. Every Swiss body of any significance is made up of all four major ones – CVP (catholic), FDP (capitalist), SP (socialist with a tinge of green) and SVP (stuff the EU, chuck out foreigners but keep their cash).

Gianni strokes my hair and I snuggle into the crook of his shoulder. I run one hand through the curls on his chest and wonder if he'd mind me shaving them off. They'd make a great wig.

"You could join one, too," Gianni says.

"I went to the Brownies once but didn't fit in. Not exactly a party person." My hand meanders down his belly and I tell myself to concentrate. Perhaps this time I'll be able to make love without seeing Max's face on the headboard.

In the morning I flop to the bathroom in languorous, post-screw mood, plonk myself on the loo and come face to face with a matt, grey metal contraption which takes up ninety per cent of the washbasin shelf.

"What's this?"

Gianni's bleary head pokes round the door. "You said you wanted music while you do your make-up."

But not this lump of tin. I wanted tiny Bang and Olufson speakers. "I need that space for my stuff. I'll put it on the floor."

"No," he says, frowning. "You won't hear it properly there."

I wait till he's in the guest shower then stow it in the cupboard.

*

I dash into the staffroom for an expresso before the first lesson to find Max sitting at the departmental pc, fingers flying over the keys.

"Doing a bit of cradle-snatching now, are we?"

"Yep. Such a pleasant change not having to fake anything."

His typing gets louder.

"And how was your evening? Pass any important motions?" He swerves the mouse up to the print icon and watches the printer spit two sheets of paper into the tray. "Definitely worth while. Thanks for asking."

*

In the oak-panelled womb of the *Rathauskeller* Geoff pours me a large glass of St Saphorin. Green-cardied, Head of Department Geoff, whose shoulder's been cried on so many times it must be mouldy and whose voice is as deep as the cache of secrets he keeps. I know his, though. In the course of a distant *rioja* evening in Zurich's Spanish *Bodega*, he said teaching was fine but what he really wanted was to be Mick Jagger and live in a haunted house.

"How're things?" he asks.

"All right, I suppose."

"No news about your Dad's operation?"

"No."

"Cheese and olives to go with the wine?"

"Thought you were on a diet?" The same one he's been on since I met him twenty-six years ago at North London Poly.

"No," he laughs. "I've resigned myself to looking like this. I love food and I'm fed up with depriving myself of it."

He asks for a Chästeller – a selection of Swiss and French cheeses, bread and olives. When the waitress arrives, he pushes it to the middle of the table. "Help yourself."

"No, thanks."

"Not long to go now." He spreads a thick layer of butter over rough brown bread, tops it with a scoop of runny, gold Vacherin d'Or and pops it into his mouth.

My mouth waters. "What?"

"Interview for the headship. Got to think of next year's timetable, advertise for someone to take over your lessons." He smiles ruefully. "Or Max's, God forbid."

"Suppose so."

"You're looking remarkably calm, under the circs."

"Haven't really got time to get nervous."

He pours us both another glass of wine. "Wish you'd have some of this cheese. It's wonderful. We've known each other a long time now, haven't we?"

"Yes?"

"Can I ask you something, Val? You don't have to answer, of course."

I smile. There's not much I wouldn't tell him. "Fire away."

"Well, I must admit I was a bit surprised when I heard you'd applied."

"Think I'm not up to it?"

He laughs and shakes his head. "I was surprised, that's all. Didn't think you'd be interested."

"Well, I am."

"Really?"

"Wouldn't have applied if I weren't, would I?"

"So it's got nothing to do with Max wanting it?"

"Not everything in my life is connected to That Man."

"All right, all right, keep your wig on. I was only asking."

*

"You know that coat's full of holes?"

"Give me your hand and belt up," Paul laughs. "You're only narked because I've dragged you out."

I put my hand in his, lift the hem of my Max Mara coat and hike one Bally-booted foot over the stile. When he met me at the hospital gate and said we couldn't see Dad, they were doing some tests, I thought we'd pound the well-tended pavements of The Ridgeway. I wasn't prepared for the wilds, even if it is only Enfield.

"It's got holes in it, that coat. And the hem's coming down."

"Adds to its character," Paul says. "Banker's overcoat, this. Best quality gear. Got it in a Heart Foundation shop up town." He reaches down into navy wool depths. "One of the pockets is torn. Stuff keeps falling through." He pulls out a packet of cigarettes and lights one, holding the smoke in his lungs long enough to clog every capillary.

"You're probably the wrong person to ask," I start, "but I can't sit back and say nothing."

Paul screws up his eyes. "What about?"

"Can't you tell Dad not to smoke?"

"You tell him," Paul says. "If it bothers you that much."

"He'll listen to you. He won't take any notice of me or Mum."

He looks at the end of his cigarette, takes one last drag, drops the butt on the path and squashes it into the dirt. "I'm not telling him, Val. What else has he got to live for?"

"Should have known the smokers would stick together. What about Bart's?"

He shrugs. "If he gets there."

"Have you been talking to the doctors? Do you know something I don't?"

"No," he says, giving my shoulder a squeeze. "Look, Val, that's all he looks forward to, his trip to the potting shed for a couple of stogies."

"But they're killing him."

"And you think he'll stop if I tell him?"

"Dunno, but it's worth a try, surely?"

We walk on in silence. Cows moo in a field far too near. "How are things at the centre?"

"Gives me a real buzz. Never thought I'd say that of a job."

"What about money, though? I know you're not getting paid." I look at his coat. "You could give me your account number. I could transfer some cash."

"No need," he says. "Got a job at that new restaurant in the parade of shops near the flat."

"Doing what?"

"Dishwasher."

I force myself to smile and nod.

"I know it's not much," he says, "but it's dosh. And I'm sick of being on the dole."

"But it…"

"Yeah?"

"It'll ruin your hands."

He laughs. "You'll have to do better than that."

"You won't have time to do your volunteer work, then they'll never offer you a job."

"I'll work at the centre during the day, do the restaurant in the evenings."

"But I could help."

He lights up another cigarette. "No. Thanks, Val, but no."

You're as stubborn as your father, I think, as we plod on. "What about Dad's operation? What do you really think?"

"'Cos of the stroke, you mean?" He shrugs. "It's what he wants. The surgeon says it'll give him another ten years. Dad believes him."

"What do you feel, though? Will he get through it?" I've got nil intuition but there's something comfortingly spooky about Paul.

"Dunno. Honest. Let's wait and see." He sets his jaw, the same as Dad does. The same as I do.

"And what's happening on the woman front? We haven't had a chance to chat for ages what with all Dad's stuff."

"Same old crap. The ones I'd really go for just want me as a friend. Mind you, I think one of the nurses at the centre might fancy me."

"Ask her out, then. What are you waiting for?"

"Can't."

"Why the hell not?"

"Haven't got the dosh."

I put my hand through the crook of his arm. "You don't have to pay for women anymore. We're in the twentieth century, for God's sake."

"If I go out with a woman, I want to."

"But think of all the chances you miss. You might meet the love of your life, she'd gladly take you out but you won't go 'cos you think you have to pay. It's mad."

"The right woman'll come along at the right time."

"Maybe there is no right one. Maybe there's just messy human muck and you have to make the best of it."

"I won't settle for second best," he says. "I'd rather be on my own."

I stand on tiptoe and kiss his cheek. He opens a farm gate, ushers me onto tarmac, back to the civilised world.

*

I push open the hospital door and dawdle through warm, antiseptic fug. I've spent thirty king-size minutes mingling with dressing-gowned smokers at the main entrance, waiting for Paul, who's just phoned to say he can't come. Someone's called in sick and he's off to the centre. Might as well go in now I'm here. At least I'll be in the warm.

Dad looks up from his rubbishy war novel. "On your own to-day?"

"Yep. You'll have to make do with me."

He screws up his face. "Oh, don't say that, dear."

I give him a box of Terry's All Gold and sit down. "Have you lost weight, Dad?"

"No, still the same as I've always been."

He's lying. You could draw a skull just from looking at his head.

He tears off the wrapper and bends the lid back to read which chocolate is which. "My favourites, these." He takes one and pops it into his mouth. He chews for a minute, takes the chocolate out of his mouth, looks round for somewhere to put it. I hand him a tissue.

"Sorry, dear. Can't eat it. It's too hard for my dentures."

"What have you been up to?" he asks.

I might as well play along. It'll pass the time. "Well, there's been a lot on at school. Did Mum tell you I've applied for the Head's job?"

His eyes wander off, attracted by the swish of curtains, the rattle and squeak of trolleys.

"Dad, are you listening?"

He looks at me, wide-eyed, mouth slightly open, and I realise he's not doing it on purpose.

A young girl, swift and sprightly in a pelmet miniskirt, enters the ward. Twelve watery eyes follow every step, beneath fawn or grey cardigans pacemakers go into overdrive.

"Hallo."

"Hallo, dear," Dad replies. "How are you today? This is my daughter. Come all the way from Switzerland. Aren't I lucky?"

I blush the puce of her lip gloss.

"Lovely country," she says. "I've always wanted to go there. So clean."

"That's Charlie's granddaughter," Dad confides in a stage whisper. "Comes to see him every week."

"I've brought these with me," she shouts, taking some dog-eared photos from a designer rucksack. She holds one in front of Charlie's bemused face.

"Who's that, Grandad?"

He frowns in concentration.

Oh God. It's going to be a test. I wonder if she's a bloody teacher. "I don't know."

Leave it, I want to say. Talk to him about the weather, tell him a story. Don't set him an exam he's bound to fail.

She carries on, undeterred. "It's your son."

Charlie smiles. A dim light is dawning. "Michael?"

"No, Peter. My father."

"Yes," Charlie says, taking the photo and gazing at it fondly. "Michael's a good boy."

Peter or Michael is whisked away and replaced by another image. "And who's that?"

Dad and I are silent. Riveted.

Charlie says nothing.

"That's Claude, Gramps."

"Who's he?"

A slight gasp of irritation. "You know her, Gramps. She's my sister."

Charlie's confusion is now complete. "Yes," he whispers, voice wavering towards falsetto. "but who are you?"

"What were you saying, dear?" Dad asks. "Tell me about your new flat. Mum says it's lovely."

I give him the full estate agent's patter and get so carried away I forget myself. "I wish you could see it."

I sit, poker-backed, waiting.

His eyes fill and he clears his throat.

"I'd like to come," he says. "I'd like to see it for myself."

"You will, Dad," I say. "As soon as you're better, come over with Mum." I feel really sad saying that. Don't know why.

I don't want to blub so look round the ward for something to laugh at. On the right by the door an old man struggles to his feet, balancing tipsily on two walking sticks: a geriatric spider, blown to and fro by a breeze no-one else can feel. Every muscle in his face is strained. His tongue darts in and out of his mouth as he surveys his audience. Then he bows his head in concentration and fires off a volley of clear, crisp, military farts.

"Trapped wind," Dad sympathises. "It's the bane of our lives."

"We call him Grandad," Dad explains, "because he's 95. It was his birthday yesterday. We all got a bit of cake. Even that bastard Charlie. Even though I told Jasmine he was the one that nicked my phone."

"I need the bottle, dear," Dad says.

I jump up from my chair. "Urgently?"

"No," he says. "Not urgent, but don't hang about."

I walk over to the nurses' station, to Jasmine the carer, who's filling in a form with a frown on her face and a jumbo bar of Fruit and Nut on her desk.

"Sorry to trouble you. My Dad needs to use a bottle."

She puts down her pen and lumbers off to the sluice then draws the screen round Dad's chair with a rattle of iron rings, leaving me in no doubt whose job she thinks this is.

When she's gone back to her paperwork, Dad and I sit in comfortable silence like a real parent and child. I glance at my watch and realise it's five past four. I've been here for more than an hour. Better not push it and stay. And anyway, if I don't go now, I'll get caught in the rush hour and the twenty-minute journey'll take more than an hour.

"I'll be back tomorrow, Dad."

"All right, dear," he smiles. "I'll look forward to it."

*

"What time shall we go?" Mum asks next day when I totter down for breakfast rubbing my back – the princess and the pea.

"I was thinking of going on my own."

"Oh." Her voice is full of gentle disappointment.

"On the other hand," I say, switching on the kettle and getting two mugs from the draining board, "I'd be glad of the company."

Lying to My Family. Jesus Christ. I've got a Ph.D. in it.

*

116

Dad's in his usual chair, wearing the brown jumper I bought him at Christmas.

"Seen my new woolly?" he asks. "Nice, isn't it?"

The jumper's familiar but I don't recognise the trousers. Neither does Mum from the way she's looking at them.

"I'm not sure these are mine," Dad explains, noticing our attention's focused below his belt. "Wouldn't have to wear them if that Beverly'd got me to the bathroom in time. She might be the sister but she's not as good as Jasmine."

They all seem to have swapped their trousers. Tailoring courtesy of the fit-where-it-touches-school. Ethel, chirping *If I Ruled the World* from the depths of her comfort blanket, has got the best deal. No-one would put her skirts into the communal pool.

"Don't worry, Jack," Mum says. "I'll get some name-tags."

"Who's in the bed opposite?" I ask. The screen's tightly drawn, not an inch of space you could peek through.

"Bloke in a coma," Dad replies. "Arthur says he was here when he arrived three months ago." He gives Charlie a filthy glance. "At least he keeps quiet."

At the far end of the ward opposite Grandad, Arthur cowers in his bed while Dr Khan confers with Beverly.

"His problem is hygiene," Beverly says. "It's his faeces, doctor."

Khan nods sagely. You can tell by the look on his face he's glad he only deals with shit by proxy.

"I do try to help him," she adds, "but it's not easy."

"You know what I really fancy?" Dad says.

I shake my head.

"A fag."

"Come on, then." I start prising off his slippers. Once red, they're now mottled purple, patterned by every meal he's had here.

"No good doing that, dear," Mum says. "He can't get into his shoes."

"Bloody shrunk, the lot of them," Dad grumbles. "Help me into my anorak, would you?"

He lifts up his arms and I poke them down the sleeves.

"Now, you go one side of me," he says. "Your mum can take the other. I'm a bit wobbly on my pins today."

We steer him towards the French windows.

Grandad pipes up, "You're not going to open them, are you? Makes an awful draught."

"Don't listen to him," Dad says. "He's only jealous he can't get out."

At snail's pace we pass the gym.

"The torture chamber," Dad says. "I go every day."

I look at Mum and raise an eyebrow.

"It's true," she says. "They all have thirty minutes' physio daily."

"Pick your feet up, Dad." It would be so much easier if he didn't shuffle.

"That's what the physio tells me. 'Pick your feet up, Jack, and don't lean back otherwise you'll fall over.' Balance," he concludes, "that's my only problem."

When we get back to the ward, Dad having smoked three fags amid mulch, manure and a selection of grow-bags, there's a bustle round the bed opposite his. Beverly and Jasmine are tucking blue blankets under the mattress and plumping up pillows.

"What's going on, here?" Dad demands.

"We've moved Gerald onto a side ward," Beverly explains. "He's very poorly. You'll be getting some new company. That'll be nice for you, won't it?"

"Is that you, Meg?" Charlie whispers. "Get under the covers. Hurry up so they don't see you."

"She's not here," Dad whispers, reaching for a handful of chocolate digestives. "Run off with Hitler, I heard."

*

"Val?" Max's voice issues from the depths of a staffroom cupboard.

I turn on my heel and re-open the door.

"Hang on," he calls. "Just wanted to ask how you are. Must be tough with your Dad being ill."

"Mmm."

"How is he?"

"All right. Still waiting for a bed at Bart's."

He brushes dust from his hands. "National Health's a bummer, isn't it?"

"He's being well looked after."

"And you? Are you ok? You look tired."

I breathe in, stand up straight. "I'm fine."

"Well, I do admire you," he says, amber eyes glimmering. "Don't know if I could cope so well, 'specially with the interview and all."

"What interview?"

"Came in the mail this morning. Monday fortnight. Me at nine, you at nine forty-five."

"Oh. Yes. Of course."

Nessun Dorma tinkles from my handbag. "Sorry."

Max tuts and swishes out of the room, looking as if he'd like to give me a thousand lines.

"It's me, dear," Mum says. "I just wanted to give you the good news. We've heard from Bart's. They've got your Dad a bed. Operating in two weeks' time. Monday at nine. You can imagine how thrilled he is."

I switch off the mobile and sink into an armchair. Can't stand. My legs have gone all wobbly.

# Chapter Seven

## March 1996

### Jack

A trolley with Moby Dick in polyester bags rattles through the ward, squeaks to a stop by the bed opposite mine. I'm sitting in my chair, waiting for the off to Bart's – sharpish, soon as that ambulance arrives.

"Not going down to the dining room today, Jack?" Lily asks. Slim and dark, she is, like a mink. We call her SS Lil. Thinks she's using a Brillo pad when she washes your privates. Charlie tries to get out of it. Says, "No, thank you, Lily," in his poshest voice but she won't have it. She scrubs him down a treat.

"I'm having lunch at Bart's."

"Oh no, you're not," she says. "It'll be far too late when you get there. You eat here with your friends."

Before I can tell Lily these goons are no friends of mine, the porter at the top end of the trolley grins and says, "Right, Ronald. Let's be having you."

The whale raises his head and puffs, "I'll do my best. My name's Rinaldo, by the way."

It takes the head physio and two porters to balance him on the edge of the biggest chair on the ward. He looks across to me and smiles.

"Hallo. How are you today?"

"All right. When's my ambulance coming?"

"Whenever it gets here," Lily says. "Stop nagging, Jack, will you?"

Beverly and Lily examine the blob. They talk as if he weren't there, just like they do with the rest of us.

"He's too young for a geriatric ward, surely?" Lily wonders.

"No bed anywhere else," Beverly says. "Now, how are we going to get him into his?"

Good question. The two of them'll never manage and the physio and porters buggered off as soon as they could.

Beverly puts a finger to her lips and taps a foot. She's in crimson leggings today. Matches the Eyetie's face. Then she says, "A-ha!" and walks off with that look she gets when she's decided to give you an enema.

She comes back with a metal contraption last used in the Spanish Inquisition. "The hoist'll do it."

Lily draws the curtains round his bed. "Now, get up, Ronald," she snaps.

There's a deep sigh and the crack of straining wood.

"I can't. And please, my name's Rinaldo, not Ronald."

"Well, you'll just have to try, whatever your name is," Beverly says. "And don't fall over, either, 'cos we can't lift you."

*

Here comes Jasmine with the lunch trolley. I see Lily whispering to her, nodding in my direction.

"It's your favourite today," Jasmine says. "Tomato soup, roast chicken with all the trimmings, rhubarb crumble and custard."

"I'm not having it. I'm eating at Bart's."

"We don't know when your ambulance'll be here," she says. "There's been an accident in the City. Have a bite, go on. Just to tide you over."

The Eyetie gets a low-fat yoghurt. He spoons the carton out three times, scraping up every last dreg. If he was on his own, he'd lick it out. No bloody manners. He watches every mouthful I take and when I suck the last bit of crumble off my spoon, he licks his lips. "Been here long, have you?"

"Long enough. Leaving today."

"Going home?"

"Got to have an op first."

He winces. "Now that would worry me."

I soon put him right. "Not a bit of it. Best team in the country, my surgeon's. Best team in the world, that is. 'Course, I'd never have it done here."

He looks worried. "Not a good place, then, or what?"

"It's all right, long as you haven't got anything serious."

He frowns. "Had to come here. It's my local hospital. You live in this area?"

"Yep."

"Me, too. Dad came over to work in the nurseries. Sent for us as soon as he could."

"Much better life over here, I suppose?"

Now that sticks a harpoon in his blubber.

"No," he says, chins wobbling. "Not where I'm from. Got a very high standard of living with the tourists. Come from all over the world."

"Do they now?"

"Sea's so blue you wouldn't believe it." He picks up the plastic beaker of water Beverly's left on his table, looks at it then puts it back. "Yeah," he sighs. "Salerno. *Bella citta*."


Valerie

Strong arms grab me, press me into a black leather chest. "Where the hell have you been?" Gianni demands. "I've been going *pazzo*. You had your mobile switched off, for God's sake."

I wriggle out of his embrace. "Went to see Dad. Must have forgotten to turn it back on." Like I've forgotten a thousand other things. Brain's regressed to mono.

He follows me down the hall, too close on my heels.

"Can I get you a drink?"

He shakes his head. "No, thanks."

I pour myself another glass of *Amarone*.

He hugs me again. "Good to see you."

I wait for him to sit on the sofa, then perch on the edge of the armchair opposite. He pats the space beside him. "Come here."

"No." They're taking Dad up to Bart's today. Doing tests, getting him ready.

There's a touch of irritation in Gianni's voice. "I just want to talk."

He gazes at me, I stare at the carpet.

He gets up, walks round the coffee table, sits on the arm of my chair. One hand strokes my hair, the other slides round my shoulder. Automatically I lean against him, then straighten up. He takes hold of me, eases me back. His heart thuds against my brain.

"You're tense."

"I'm fine."

"I could help, you know."

"You can't do the interview for me and it's not your Dad under the knife."

"I know all that but I could look after you a bit. Make sure you get some decent food."

"No." The word's out before I can dilute it. "It's sweet of you and everything but I'm not hungry."

His hands drop from my shoulders. "*Dio! Devi mangiare!*"

"I said I'm not bloody hungry! Just need to be on my own for a while."

He gets up, goes to the kitchen. "Anyone else would be glad of the company."

"Well, I'm not anyone else. I don't know why you're making such a fuss."

"Think I'll have that glass of wine."

"Help yourself."

The deep red liquid bubbles into the glass. One shimmering sphere glides down the stem, settles on the marble table top. Normally I'd dash to the kitchen for a cloth but today I can't be bothered. I sit tapping my feet, waiting for him to sit down.

"No relationship stays the same, *cara*. It has to change."

"Meaning what?"

"Meaning just that. *Madre di Dio*! People do live together."

I should have seen this coming. His stuff appearing in my cupboards -rice, pasta machine, parmesan shaver, the slow insinuation of socks and pants into my bedroom. "Not now, please. I can't stand it." My voice is too harsh, too loud, but he's like Clingfilm.

His voice simmers. "I wish I knew what you want."

So do I. Oh, God, so do I. "Just need to sort myself out."

"And you think you're in a fit state to do that?" He raises his hands to the ceiling for support. "Now of all times?"

"Got to try."

He takes a half-glass slug, refills both, gets up and walks to the window. "This isn't some kind of punishment, is it? For not being around for your father's operation? Can't cancel the *Firenze* gig, *cara*, or *Roma*. I told you. They've been arranged for months."

"I know."

"Then what the hell is this about?"

How should I know? I feel like sinking into the sofa, closing the cushions over my head. Instead I fling my arms in the air, fumble for words. "I just wish, oh, I don't know, I wish you weren't always so theatrical. So... Italian!"

He stares at me as if I were a square cannelloni. "*Stronzo, Valeria,* it's what I am!"

I glare back, grateful he's angry. "What're you looking at me like that for?"

"Something's up. You're different."

"My Dad might die, for Christ's sake."

"It's not that."

He taps one suede-booted foot, stares out across the lake, then back at me. "There isn't anyone else, is there? 'Cos if there is, I'll boil his balls in extra ve*rgine*, I'll…"

He sees me crying, strides back to my chair. "Why the hell won't you let me help?"

I hold my glass towards him. "OK. Fill that up."

"*Merda!* Can't you ever be serious? Just for one moment?"

"I've got enough bloody serious at the moment," I shout. "All right?"

He stands, fists clenched in freeze-frame, then turns away. "I'd better go." His glass clanks on the table, leaves a second mark. Two overlapping circles – a pair of smudged red rings. "You know where I am. *My* mobile will be on."

He marches down the hall, slams the door.

"Good bloody riddance!" I mutter into the last glass of wine before sprinting to the balcony to see if he's coming back.

\*

"You look like a cowpat," I tell my dowager duchess outfit, then turn away from my reflection in disgust. I take one sip of tea, chuck the rest, glance at my watch yet again: five-thirty. Interview's nine forty-five. Five-thirty here, four-thirty in London. Wonder if Dad's awake and nervous, too.

I get into the car and drive round the lake four times. Bugger environmental consciousness today. Got to be busy, busy, busy!

I'm outside the conference room early enough to shake hands with the school governors, who smile at me and check their watches. Doris the dinner lady, wheels a trolley of coffee and croissants past, asks if I'd like a cup. I say no, thanks. I flick through out-of-date magazines, the school prospectus, count the leaves on the potted plants. Max flashes past at two minutes to nine, gives the door a perfunctory tap, walks straight in.

126

"Good luck," he smiles, as he holds the door open half an hour later.

Stefan Schilthorn, head governor, stands at the top of the table, hand extended. I want to walk towards him but my legs have frozen. Something's clutching my heart, crushing it as hard as the Alessi lemon squeezer I got Gianni for Christmas. "I don't think you've met our new governor," Stefan Schilthorn says. "Dr Frank Herzog."

The hair's grey not silver, eyes green not blue but the see-right-through-you gaze is the same as Dad's, likewise the lightning-rod posture. His suit's a double of the silver grey Boss Dad wore for my wedding. I sit, straight-backed on the chair, telling myself not to be so bloody stupid. This isn't Dad. He's a thousand miles away.

Stefan Schilthorn coughs into his hand. "Perhaps I might begin. What do you consider to be your greatest strengths and weak-nesses?"

"I'm a good teacher, I think. I am strict but I get results. The vast majority of my pupils pass their finals."

Frau Steiner, crew-cutted, trouser-suited founder of the *Frauen-zentrale,* the Women's Advisory Centre, purses shiny maroon lips. "And those that don't?"

"I give my classes all the help I can but I can't learn grammar and vocabulary for them. They have to make some effort them-selves."

Stefan Schilthorn nods. His charcoal suit, droopy moustache and limpid eyes make him look like a seal. "I don't think anyone doubts your qualities as a teacher What I'd like to hear about are abilities you feel would make you a good head."

"I'm determined. I carry projects through, don't give up easily." A plodder, Dad once said. I hated him for it, wanted to be sparkly and mercurial. "And I'm straightforward. What you see is what you get."

Dad smiles. No, Frank Herzog. I clench my fists. Pull yourself together, woman.

"You say what you think?" he says.

Freesias on the table. Like my bouquet. But I had roses. Cerise. Dad's buttonhole.

*'I've never seen your father so proud as your wedding day.'*

"Yes, well. I'm not sure. I..."

"Let's move on," Frank Herzog says. "We can come back to that later. What's your ideal style of management?"

"Um, open mind. I mean, open door. Staff and pupils must feel they can pop in whenever they've got a problem."

"And how would you describe your communication skills?" He twiddles a black Mont Blanc biro. His fingers are long, slender, nails well-tended. No wedding ring. Just like Dad.

"Ms Sterling?"

A tremor in my voice stretches one syllable to two. "Goo-ood."

"You don't sound terribly sure?" Frau Steiner cocks her hedgehog head.

"No, No. I am. I, er, just think they could be improved. Like anybody's. I mean, who communicates as well as they'd like? Nobody. I mean, I don't know anybody. Do you?" A sickly laugh slips through my lips and dies.

Frau Steiner raises one eyebrow. "Quite."

Frank Herzog gives me a sympathetic smile.

Stefan Schilthorn knits his brow. "The post of Head is quite demanding, as I'm sure you realise. How would you cope with the stress?"

An irate hedgehog and a seal are asking me if I can deal with strain. Makes me want to giggle.

"Yes?" Stefan Schilthorn and Frau Steiner lean forward, waiting for a tit-bit.

I bow my head, tense every muscle in my torso to strangle that laugh. "I've spent the past three months commuting between Zug and London. I've not missed one lesson. I think that proves something."

Stefan Schilthorn tugs at his moustache. "Everything all right in London, I hope?"

"Yes. Well, no." I look at Frank Herzog, return his smile, tear my eyes away. "It's my father. He's ill."

The rest of the interview passes in a blur. I sit, waiting to be dismissed, knowing I've blown it. Stuttered like a zombie, giggled like a moron, couldn't take my eyes off a school governor – that should just about do it.

As I shuffle out of the conference room, I fix my eyes on the stubbled grey carpet.

"You all right?" Max asks.

Think I might throw up in one of the pot plants. "Yeah, fine."

He's near enough for me to smell his aftershave – *Egoiste*, smells like. He moves closer still, pats my shoulder. "You don't look it." He nods towards the study. "How did it go?"

"It's not that."

"Your dad?"

I ferret in my bag for one of the half-used tissues that tangle with my Filofax. Max hands me an immaculate white lawn square and I dab at my eyes, hoping some mascara's still in place and I'm not doubling as the Ghost of Christmas Past.

"You're in no fit state to drive. I'll run you home."

"Let me phone the hospital."

"No news," the ward sister says. "He's still down in theatre. It's a long job. Why don't you call around two?"

I get into the silver Audi Dad's always wanted. Can't abide the Krauts in Majorca but they make good cars. Reckons that's the first thing he'll buy when he wins the lottery. 'I'll tell Jack Barclay to stuff the Rolls,' he says, 'I'm having the biggest Audi in the showroom.'

"How did you know about Dad's operation?"

Max lights a cigarette, presses a button and a window glides open. "Asked Geoff. Why?"

"Just wondered." I reach for the packet. "May I?"

"Help yourself."

The nicotine slams into my lungs and we race down to the lake then up to *Postplatz*, where afternoon shoppers sip cappuccino outside a steel and chrome café. We whiz past designer boutiques, skid to a halt outside the florist's on *Kolinplatz*.

"Won't be a sec," he says, jumping out of the car.

He returns with a single, pale pink rose. "Just a little cheerer-upper."

I don't trust myself to speak.

"I liked your dad."

"I know." Two of a kind.

"Remember the day we took him and your Mum to Berne?"

I nod, squash a tear that's sneaking down my cheek. "Had a good time."

He reaches over, squeezes my shoulder. "He'll be fine. Bart's is brilliant. World famous and all that."


He pulls up on one of the visitors' parking spaces and I pick up my briefcase. "Will you be all right?"

"Yes." I let go of the handle, flop back in the seat, close my eyes. "No. Dunno."

He smiles. "Could go for a coffee and then lunch?"

"Not hungry."

"Shall I come up, then? Keep you company? If nobody minds, that is."

He strolls into the flat as if he'd never left it, dumps our briefcases in the alcove by the balcony window. "Coffee?"

"Please."

He opens and closes all the right doors. I sit at the dining table, look out across the lake at the view Dad's never seen. Max makes two expressos, adds a dash of cream to mine.

"I'll give the hospital another buzz."

Sister says no news is good news and I should phone back in an hour.

Max, shoes off, pads back into the kitchen. "More coffee?"

"No. Open a bottle of *Montepulciano*. Bloody coffee's making me nervous."

As he puts the glass down, I grab his wrist. He pulls me to my feet, sends the coffee cup flying, pushes me against the wall, one hand yanking down my tights. No time to take them off. We come fast, him with his usual primeval shout, me with a long, low moan.

"Want me to go?" he whispers.

"No."

"Just heard from theatre," Sister Julia says. "They're keeping him for a while. His temperature's dropped."

My voice wavers. "Is that serious?"

"Nothing to worry about. They wrap them in tin foil, wait for it to go up again. Often happens after these long ops, dear."

"I'll ring in an hour."

"Good," she soothes. "I'm sure he'll be back by then."

We pass the time in bed.

"Didn't fake that, did you?"

"No. You've got your faults but that's not one of them."

"Thank God for that," he says. "Couldn't stand it if you started, too."

I reach across the bedside table to the phone, dial the hospital number. "Come on, you lazy shits."

"Percival Potts ward, Sister Julia speaking."

"Valerie Sterling."

"They've just brought him up, dear. The operation was a complete success. Mr Macbeth's very pleased."

Max and I are, too. We celebrate horizontally.

# Jack

Sweating like a carthorse, balls itching. Look down at my legs. Bloody serge. Scrapes like a loofah. Not a patch on the Yanks' uniforms.

Beachmaster's voice booms, "Come on, that Dodge."

Bump, bump, off ramp. Stuck in bloody Italian sand. Be all right, though. Bulldozers'll pull us out. Then shelling starts.

"Fucking fuckers are fucking shooting at us!" Alf screams.

Someone's put a match to Enfield arms factory. Noise so solid our hearts beat to it. Beach blasts up, a wall of sea looms. Foot jammed on the accelerator. "Move, you fucker, move!"

Shelling fades. Just about make out a voice from shore. "Come on in. You're covered."

Our lot or the Krauts? Christ knows.

Dugout sand's damp. Makes me shiver. Choke on stink of cordite. Fags! God help my fags! Senior Service. Won off Alf at poker. Buggered if I'm losing them. Going mad with noise. Sobbing Sisters, Brens, Kraut machine guns. Shells make the ground quake. Stuff fingers in my ears. Come out red. Shake helmet, blink sand from eyes. Clouds of black smoke. Yellow flashes. Infernal noise. Going on forever. Nothing but noise and more bloody noise.

Crawl out, pick up shreds of cloth, empty feet, boots.

"Found another finger," Alf says.

"Not a finger," sergeant says. Holds out ration box.

Alf's breakfast comes up in a perfect arc.

Hand him Senior Service. "Game wasn't fair. You're bloody useless at poker."

Can't sleep. Bloody Alf's tugging at my sleeve. "Leave off, Alf, you bastard."

"It isn't Alf, Jack. It's Louise."

"Louis who? No frogs in our lot."

132

"Louise, your nurse. The morphine's making you delirious. You've been yelling your head off, upsetting all the others. You feeling all right?"

I wipe my eyes and hope she'll go away. "I'm fine."

## Valerie

I plod along Bart's corridor, trying to push Max out of my mind. I want him in Switzerland, where he belongs but the bugger won't stay put. He keeps popping up in my head as fast as we fell into bed Max Heineken – reaching the parts other men don't.

Two young nurses, one auburn, one brunette, sit at a battered desk filling in charts. I see what Dad means about the staff: caps stiff as royal icing, immaculate uniforms, stockings the thick liquorice real nurses wear. I walk up to the redhead, who raises a Royal Doulton face.

"Can I help you?"

"I'm looking for my father. Mr Sterling."

"Jack's over there," she smiles. "Second on the left."

That skin-covered skeleton bears no resemblance to my father but I don't want to offend her so walk across to make sure. Jesus Christ, it is him! He's on a drip, arms straight at his sides as if practising to be a corpse. I take his hand and squeeze it. No reaction.

I'm sniffling quietly to myself when the nurse comes round to take his temperature.

She puts a hand on my shoulder. "You all right?"

"He's dying, isn't he?"

"Goodness, no, love," she says. "He seems a lot worse than he is. That's all."

"But he's so thin, such an awful colour."

"Oh, my dear," she smiles, "he's looked one helluva lot worse than he does today."

He opens his eyes, blinks and yawns.

"Shall I come back in half an hour? Give you time to wake up?"

"No," he says through another yawn. "Just had a little nap."

He looks me up and down. "You look nice. Lost weight?"

"Yes. You have, too."

"No. Don't think so."

I glance at the metal tray on his bedside table. "What's that?"

He pulls a face. "My lunch."

"Hope you ate it." I lift the scarred plastic plate warmer, see brown lumps in gravy thick as school dinner custard and shudder.

He inspects one of his hands and tuts. "Look at the state of these nails. Bloody disgrace."

"I could do them for you."

He smiles. "That'd be nice."

I take one hand, rest it on mine. The skin is tough; a testament to his three score and ten but below the surface there's warmth. Dark hilly veins lead to slim, sparsely-haired fingers that have an elegance about them, as if he was meant to lead a better life. I take his other hand and clip the nails. Grey flakes fall onto the blanket. I put down the clippers and his hand stays on mine for a second. As he goes to pull away, I hold on to his fingertips. "Not done yet. Let me file them, do the cuticles."

"All right." His voice is shaky, eyes brimming.

He sniffs, looks me up and down. "Hardly ever see you in a dress. Should wear them more often. You've got good legs. Like me."

His vanity makes me smile. Dad's got the worst case of bees' knees I've ever seen. "You're getting calluses here. I'll put some cream on."

He surveys the other patients, who are playing a symphony of muted snores. "No-one to talk to here."

"Mmm." I rub each finger thoroughly with Age-Defying hand cream.

He frowns. "Suppose school keeps you busy. All that marking. Can't have time for much else?"

I smile and wink. His wink when he slipped me extra pocket money unbeknown to Mum. "I manage."

A brief sparkle lights up his eyes. "You have a bit of fun while you can." He holds out his hands, turns them once, twice, smiles. "Thank you, dear."

His eyes close and he smiles again, weaker this time. I squeeze his hand and silently leave the ward.


## Jack

The porter pushes me back onto Bramley in a wheelchair.

"Last bed on the right," Jasmine smiles. "Kept it warm for you. And you're just in time for lunch."

Arthur waves. "Good to see you, mate." Charlie fiddles with his flies as usual. Grandad lowers the Financial Times. "Everything go all right?"

Jasmine helps me into my armchair and pulls up the table.

The Eyetie's eyes nearly pop out of his head. "That looks good."

"Not really fond of foreign food but I don't mind a bit of lasagne now and again."

He looks as if he's going to burst into tears. "Sauce looks creamy. Lot of cheese, too."

"What are you having?"

"Chicken broth and crispbread. What I'd really like is a plate of *spaghetti alle vongole*."

"What's that when it's at home?"

"Clams. Mama used to say, Rinaldo, you go to the quay, wait for the fishermen. Pick out the best *vongole* for me. Wonderful."

"Don't eat seafood. Gives my belly gip."

"If you lived on the coast, you would. Ever been to Italy, Jack?"

"No. Well, once. Long time ago."

"You should go back. It's beautiful. You could visit my family. I'd tell them. They'd make you very welcome."

All of a sudden I feel knackered. Trek in the ambulance must have tired me out. Might get some shut-eye. Just for a minute or two. I look across at the Eyetie. His eyes are still on my tray.

"Have it if you like. It's too much for me. Haven't touched the sponge pudding."

He beams.

"You'll have to come and get it, though."

He checks the coast is clear, rolls himself out of bed and is at my side faster than he's ever moved for the physio.

As I drift off to sleep, Beverly's voice floats through the ward.

"How're you doing Ronald? Getting used to your diet?"

"Oh, yes," the cheeky sod says. "Starting to feel really well on it."

Rinaldo, I think. His name's not Ronald. It's Rinaldo.

Valerie

I'm surrounded by thick black darkness. I know I'm outside – I can feel the ground under my feet – but I can't see it. There are no stars, not a speck of light. I've always hated the dark but I'm not afraid now, even though I know I'm very, very small. My tiny right paw is wrapped in a giant hand. Totally safe. Nothing and no-one will ever get to me as long as I've got this hand. I don't need to look up. I know who the hand belongs to: Dad.

I wake up and turn over, almost expect to see his face on the pillow, but there's just the dent from Mum's head and the smell of the lavender oil she tips over her pillowcase. I slide out of bed, stumble to the bathroom and shower the dream away.

\*

When I walk onto the ward, Jasmine's sitting at his bedside holding his hand. I stop dead. My Dad doesn't hold hands with adults. I've never seen him do it with Mum, only with Paul when he had flu. They don't see me till I'm right behind her.

"Oh," Dad says. "What a wonderful surprise."

Jasmine turns and smiles. Big fat face, big white teeth. "Catch you later, Jack. Thanks."

I plant a kiss on a craggy cheek. "What's all that about?"

"Nothing that would interest you."

"Oh?"

"Just putting her straight on a few things. Work for college."

He never helped me, not once all the time I was at school or uni. Might have been doing nuclear physics for all he knew. I scrape the visitor's chair up to his bed, sit as close as I can.

"How are you?"

"So-so, dear. Better when Jasmine's on."

I grunt, look down at my tights, notice there's a great big hole at the side of one knee. Must have snagged them getting out of the cab.

He squints at me. "You look edgy. Something bothering you?"

"Been busy, that's all." I glance at his wrinkled hand. Could hold it but I don't.

"We've had a rough time, too," he says. "A lot of them have had the flu. Jasmine's been rushed off her feet. Gets all the rotten jobs, being a carer."

Not even qualified. Probably too thick to get through the exams.

I don't stay long. On the way out I pass Jasmine scrawling in a dog-eared notebook, tongue sticking out of the corner of her mouth.

"Great you're here," she says. "You do him a power of good. Talks about you all the time."

I march up the corridor, heels stabbing the floor with each step. Behind my back my father talks to that great fat dollop of lard. About me. How bloody dare they?

# Chapter Eight

## April 1996

### Valerie

I walk into the conference room, reminding myself which country I'm in. It's not important that Max is going to get the job, I tell myself. Not life or death.

Stefan Schilthorn smiles, fiddles with his red bow tie. "I thought I'd see you both together. I do hope you don't object?"

Max smirks like a heavyweight champ. I shrug, stifle a yawn and pray he doesn't gloat too much.

"If you'll bear with me, I'd like to give you an idea of the points we considered before coming to a decision." Schilthorn nods at me. "Now, some members of the board felt it was high time we had a female Head."

I sit up straight, shoulders back. Maybe I've still got a chance.

He pauses, glances at Max. "But that should never be the main criterion." A swift left hook lands straight on my jaw.

"Ms Sterling has, of course, been with us for some considerable time."

I'm up and bouncing back.

"And has gone to the considerable trouble of doing a Swiss degree."

I float like a butterfly, sting like a bee.

"Of course, we couldn't possibly employ anyone without that qualification."

I'm beginning to hate the man, sitting there in his charcoal, chain-store suit. Why the hell can't he just get on with it?

"You've made it very difficult for us, very difficult, indeed," he says, as if it's our fault they've had to use their brain cells. "So, after long and earnest deliberation, we've come to what we feel is a fair Swiss compromise."

What's he going to do? Sack us both and give the job to a rank outsider?

Schilthorn frowns and clasps his hands. "As you know, the present Head is retiring due to ill health. We're keen to ensure that never happens again and have therefore decided to introduce job-sharing. First school in Switzerland to do so, by the way. If you accept, you'll each be responsible for seven departments. That way you'll still do some teaching and stay in touch with what's going on at ground level."

He smiles graciously at Max, then me. I beam back, thrilled. I haven't lost face, have gained someone to whinge with, share the good times and crap. We've always worked well together. Maybe that's what we were meant to do all along.

The smile on Max's face has set like school dinner custard. "Who'll represent the school at official functions?"

"We thought you might take turns, rather like the President of the Federal Council."

Max nods, a short sharp bow of the head.

I grasp Stefan Schilthorn's hand and shake it till his dentures rattle.

Geoff's waiting outside along with *Frau Hagenbüchle*, who's holding a pewter tray. When he sees the grin on my face, he dashes over and plants a big wet kiss on my lips. *Frau Hagenbüchle* nearly drops dear Stefan's hot chocolate. After shaking Max's hand, Geoff pushes me gently down the corridor. "I've booked at the *Rathauskeller*. My treat. Got to get in with the new boss."

*

The steep grass slope down to the water is dotted with daffs, the fields on the far side of the lake are yellow green. We sit at the front table, collars pulled tight to our necks but loath to be inside.

We're treating ourselves to a drink, Max and I, now we've decided who'll be in charge of what. Arts me, Economics him, Sciences split down the middle. I am calm, civilised, professional. No wondering aloud if and when we'll hit the sack, no bitchy comments re Anita, of whom I'm not jealous at all.

"Got some news," he says, idly watching a pair of swans skate the surface as they land. "Looks like I might be moving out."

Somewhere very close an atom bomb explodes and a mushroom cloud swells above Oberwil. "Oh."

His amber eyes target mine, home in. "Should never have married in the first place."

You're telling me.

He gulps down the rest of his beer, bangs his glass on the table. "Better go. Don't want to burden you with all my crap."

I watch him leave, wave as he gets into his car and doodle on a paper serviette: *Mrs Valerie Fuchs.*

\*

"You can't," Geoff insists, opening his city-gent's umbrella against the watery snow. "You'll be asking for it."

I hook three bulging carriers onto his free hand. "Well, I am, aren't I? Asking for it, I mean."

We slither up the hill to my place, the only sound our middle-aged lungs fighting for air.

"Coming in for a drink?"

"Quick coffee." He shakes the umbrella, relieves me of my shopping, takes the brace of bags into the kitchen. "I just hate seeing you set yourself up to be hurt again."

"I won't be."

He tuts at the price of Moet. "I mean, what's the guy got, for God's sake?"

I take a packet of wild rice from a bag, put it to one side for later. "He's strong, for one thing. I want someone to lean on. I'm sick of always being the boss." I switch on the expresso machine, put two cups on the tray, press the button. "Cream and sugar?"

"No cream, three sweeteners. So he's strong. What else?"

"He's intelligent."

"Granted." He takes a sip of coffee.

"Can be charming."

A splutter turns into a coughing fit. "As an anaconda. Think I will have some cream after all. Any biscuits?"

"Packet of crispbread in the cupboard. The thing is, all the feelings are still there. Wouldn't have jumped into bed with him if they weren't."

He covers two crispbread with a half-inch layer of low-fat spread. "You don't think you might be confusing lust with love?" He licks spread off a finger, wrinkles his nose. "What I'd like to know is, would he be sniffing round if you'd got the job and he hadn't?"

I finish my expresso, slot cup and saucer into the dishwasher. "Don't want to be rude but I've got to get on."

I kiss Geoff's cheek and close the door, shaking my head at the sheer bloody cheek of him. "'Course he would," I mutter to myself. 'Course he would."


This dinner is going to be perfect. I made three lists, checked ingredients, ticked them off with my red marking pen. I rinse the salmon fillet, tweezer every bone, stuff it with butter, currants, jewels of stem ginger, wrap in puff pastry and put it in the fridge to rest. I'm not doing beef like our first date. Don't eat meat anymore.

I apply my first face mask (cleansing) then shave – underarm, legs, pussy. He likes his women smooth. I'm just making an effort, not pandering to his taste. I remove the mask, apply the next (moisturising), lie in the bath and cover my eyes with stress-relief pads. After the required five minutes, I smear on the third mask (lifting) and slick myself eel-smooth with body lotion – Lancôme's Ô – a sound I'm planning to make frequent use of tonight. I dress carefully, black stockings and a whisper of Chanel that cost this month's salary. I wait with baited breath, tense as the straps on my Wonderbra.

"That looks terrific," he smiles. The pastry's gold, dill sauce whisked to perfection, parisienned potatoes worthy of Masterchef. He cuts into the pastry, puts a mouthful onto his fork, holds it up to the light. "What's this?"

"Salmon. Why?"

"I don't eat fish."

"You used to."

"Gone off it." He pushes the plate away. "Had some dodgy mussels in Provence."

"Could have told me."

"You could have asked."

There's something about beans on toast that takes the glamour out of vintage Moet. He leans back from the table and fiddles with his shoelaces. "It's good to be here. You know how much I value your company."

Enough to marry someone else. Mustn't be a cow, though. Anyone can make a mistake. We're both wiser. And older. His nose now sprouts a small but strident forest, a double chin blossoms over his denim collar. And that preppy gear doesn't suit him anymore. Far too young for a forty-year-old. Wonder if he's thinking the same about my mini.

"Shall we sit somewhere more comfortable?" It's not that I want to get my leg over right away but he's drumming his nails on the table and it's driving me mad.

We move to the sofa, sit like bookends. He fills my glass and I empty it in one. "I'm glad we're not fighting anymore," I say.

"I've never wanted to *fight* you."

"Like the dress?"

"Mmm." His smile is vulpine. "Bit daring, though. Can see your knickers."

Now that would be a miracle. I'm not wearing any.

He lights a cigarette, takes a long, deep lungful.

Wish he wouldn't do that without asking. Nobody's smoked here since I packed up.

"We've always had enormous potential," he says.

Yep, I think, I've been dreaming about yours a lot.

"Would make a great team."

I lean across, flash him an eyeful of cleavage.

"Let me do that." He takes the champagne bottle, brushes my fingers. "You might have to change your lifestyle a bit, though." He looks at my dress, critically this time. "Perhaps not spend so much on clothes. Travel more modestly."

Randy as an Easter bunny, I'm generous to a fault. "'Course. You'll have to pay alimony."

I'm just about to go for the goodies when he stops me in my tracks.

"Of course you'll have to get rid of this flat," he says, eyes scanning the room. "Far too small for the pair of us."

He can't be serious. This is my home. The first place in Switzerland that's ever meant anything. I wouldn't change a pillowcase, a cushion, not even a dishcloth, let alone move. My mind flicks back to his office, us working out who'd take which departments. He decided, took it for granted I'd agree. Just as he's doing now.

"You don't seem very enthusiastic."

"I thought you might need some space. Want to live on your own for a while."

He snorts. "Not me. Not made for it."

"It might do you good."

"Thanks, Mum."

"I don't want to be your mother."

"Then don't give me advice I don't need."

144

I take an angry gulp of champagne. "Don't want to be a seamless replacement for Anita, either."

"Christ, you are ridiculous sometimes. You're not replacing anyone."

"I just don't want to be your bloody babysitter, that's all."

We sit, glaring into our glasses. The champagne's flat now, bubbles gone.

"Want me to go?"

"Perhaps you'd better."

He kisses me on the cheek. "I don't intend to live on my own Val. Think about it."

I watch him saunter down the stairs then force myself back into the flat before I yell at him to come back. I tip what's left of the champagne down the sink, rip off the suspender belt, chuck it onto my bed. It leaves a deep, red groove in my belly.

\*

I'm sitting in Café Speck, eyeing up a *Diplomat* – confectioner's custard on a bed of booze-soaked sponge – when my mobile rings.

"It's me," says Gianni.

"Oh. How did the gigs go?"

"Great. You haven't phoned."

"Been busy." Can he hear the guilt? Sense I was screwing Max before the stamp in his passport was dry? A metallic whine bores into my skull and the line goes dead. While I'm rooting in my bag for his number, the phone rings again. "What happened?"

"*Stronzo di telefonino.* Got cut off."

"Thought you'd hung up."

"Would I phone you from *Roma* to hang up on you? *Dio, cara,* use your brain."

In the background I hear voices and the blaring of car horns. "Where the hell are you?"

"*Piazza di Spagna.* By the steps. Always a lot of tourists here. How's your father?"

"Operation went well but he's really weak."

"I'm sorry." He pauses. "Could come back. I was going to spend a few days here, see my family but…"

"I don't know."

"*Merda,*" he snaps. "You know your trouble? You put up a wall, keep people out. It's impossible to have a relationship with you."

I fiddle with a sachet of sugar, turn it upside down. "Maybe you're right."

"What?" he shouts. "Can't hear you."

"I just…" I bow my head, start to cry. "I just feel so shitty."

"Look, this line's *impossibile.* Do you want me to come back? Yes or no?"

"Yes," I sniff, grateful I don't have to be alone.

It takes all of ten minutes for airy relief to turn to stodgy certainty. I ring him back. Don't give him a chance to speak. I can't use him as a crutch. Mustn't. Not anymore.

"*Kann ich Ihnen helfen?*" the waitress inquires, watching me wipe my eyes. I shake my head. "*Nein, danke.*" Got to do it myself, I think, as she walks away. Got to help myself.

## Jack

That Jasmine's a right one, drawing the screen round the Eyetie's bed all the time. Nights mostly, after lights out. I hear them laughing, happy as pigs in muck. Bedsprings creak a bit. Not that I think there's any malarkey. The bed wouldn't take it. Had to be reinforced for the Eyetie, it couldn't stand her as well. I tackled her about it this morning but she just smiled, said I was imagining things. "Nobody else hears a sound," she said.

"That's 'cos I'm the only one awake." The rest of them are drugged up to the eyeballs.

"I have to tidy Rini's bed for him. He gets it in a right state."

I could have sworn she was blushing.

"You don't tidy up here every five minutes."

She waddled up to me, patted my hand. "That's 'cos you're neat. You never make a sow's ear of anything."

No, I thought, not much I don't. "Is he married?"

She put on her pretend frown. "None of your business."

"Just thinking of you. My pillows could do with plumping while you're here."

She sat me up, bashed them about a bit. "You all right?" she said. "Not going to keel over?"

"'Course not. I'm not Grandad."

He's always falling out of bed. Doesn't make a racket, just a gentle *fludge,* like a sack of old clothes. Jasmine picks him up, chucks him back. Wasted as a carer, that girl. If she wasn't doing her studying, she could get a job on the telly wrestling. Jasmine the Black Bomber. She'd beat hell out of the lot of them. She already wears the leggings, bloody awful things. "They do nothing for you," I say. "Make you look like Max Wall."

She gives me one of her looks. "Max who?"

Before her time. Most things I remember are.


"There now," she said, when she'd done. "Happy?"

"Old enough to be your father, he is."

She laughed and shook her head, looked over to the Eyetie's bed with a daft grin on her face. "I never knew my Dad, but Gran used to say he was tall and slim. A looker. Nothing like Rini. Now pack it in, Jack, will you?"


Stella and Valerie wouldn't believe me. They didn't say so but you could see it written all over their faces. Silly old coot. Doesn't know his arse from his elbow. They think I'm brain-dead but I see what's going on – the staff nipping off for fags when they think no-one's looking, smoking at the end of my bed 'cos they know I fancy one but can't get out to the shed. 'Specially at night. Even Jasmine. Puffs the smoke right in my face, she does. Makes me livid.

*

"Not asleep yet?"

"No," I say. "How do you expect me to get off with all this noise going on?"

Jasmine laughs. Big, hearty chuckle. Used to get my goat. I quite like it now.

"I don't suppose you do The Famous Grouse on the National Health?"

"You'd have to get someone to smuggle it in for you," she says. "What about your daughter?" In the dim light her face is like a big pumpkin – warm and jolly, a bright candle burning inside.

"No. Valerie plays by the rules. Not like me. Gordon would, though. He'd have done anything."

"I thought your son's name was Paul." She eats a couple of my grapes. Good job. They only go brown otherwise.

"Gordon was my brother."

"Didn't know you had one."

"He died in the War."

"Oh," she says. "Sorry."

Something makes me sigh, a great bigg'un, right up from my boots.

"Miss him, do you?"

"It's not that." Then I cry. I hate blubbing in front of her but there's no way I can stop. I've done a lot of bawling since the operation. Must have sprung a leak. "He shouldn't have died at all."

She pulls a wad of tissues out of her pocket. "What?"

"Nothing."

She smiles. "You might as well tell me now."

I don't know why I'm doing this. I just have to. The words won't stay inside anymore. "He wanted to serve abroad. He was always going on about seeing the Continent. Dad was dead against it, even though a mate of his reckoned he could wangle Gordon a soft job. away from the action."

She frowns. "Don't see what it's got to do with you."

"I was the one he'd have listened to. He looked up to me, Christ knows why. He did write, tell me he was going to volunteer for overseas service. The letter was redirected. Dad hadn't told him where I was."

"Somewhere secret, was it?"

"Glasshouse. The military prison at Aldershot. Had a bit of a barney with a sergeant." I wait for the look of disgust that never left Dad's face when he saw me, but she's still smiling. "By the time I got the letter, I was at infantry training centre. I didn't open it straight away. The writing was my father's, we weren't speaking. I didn't want to read how I'd disgraced the family, being court-martialled. When I finally got round to it, he'd already been posted to India. He only joined the Gunners because of me egging him on."

"But you can't blame yourself, Jack."

"If I'd written straight off, he'd have come to his senses. I know he would. He got killed, I survived. Doesn't seem right."

"Haven't got any Scotch," she says, squeezing my hand and getting off the bed, "but I'll ask doctor for something to help you sleep."

*

"I can walk all right." No-one listens. They don't when you're in a wheelchair. They talk over your head as if it's your brain playing up not your legs. Off we go – Jasmine pushing, Paul and Stella each side like prison warders. Jasmine parks me by an office door. There's a queue of people but we go right up the front, no messing.

She pats my shoulder. "See you later, Jack."

"What's all this, then?"

"I told you yesterday," Stella says. "You're going to see the social worker."

She didn't say a dicky bird but I'm not arguing. She's looking nervy and it doesn't do to upset her when she's in one of her moods.

"You all right, Dad?" Paul says.

"I don't know why you have to be here, son. You could be doing something useful." Out looking for a job instead of that volunteer lark, though it's done Stella the power of good having him around.

Alice, the social worker's name is: nicely made-up, smart black suit. Mid-thirties, I'd say.

"Now, Jack," she says, opening a folder. "As you know, we're here to discuss your future. I'm sure you realise you won't be able to stay with us indefinitely."

"I'm not planning to." That makes Stella laugh. "Soon as I'm back on my feet, I'm off."

"Of course."

I bet she doesn't live round here, not with that accent. Oakwood maybe, or Brookman's Park. "But you've had major surgery and it'll take you a while to recover."

"I know all that. I'll stay here till I'm better."

"The thing is, we might be needing your bed. I'm afraid they're in rather short supply."

"I'll go home, then."

"That would be the ideal solution, naturally, but it might be difficult for your wife." She smiles at Stella. "I know you suffer from arthritis. It's no easy option, taking care of a convalescent."

"I realise that," Stella says, "but if he wants to come home, he can. What help would I get?"

Brings tears to my eyes, that, but I'm not crying in front of bloody Alice.

"We could arrange for someone to help in the mornings," Alice says, "and put him to bed at night. But the rest of the time you'd be on your own. Do you have a downstairs lavatory?"

"No." It almost sounds as if Stella's apologising.

Alice scribbles in the file with a silver fountain pen. "We could probably arrange some money towards a stair lift."

"I'll be walking up and down right as rain." I'm not taking charity from this stuck-up moo.

"As far as I understand," she says, "the operation was on your aorta. Not to aid your balance. And we don't want you falling, do we?"

Paul squeezes my arm. "Let them put in a lift, Dad. Mum can't hold you if you fall. What are you going to do if I'm out? Lie on the floor all night?"

I suppose he's right. "If it'll help Stella."

"And it might be more convenient to have his bed downstairs," Alice says. "You wouldn't have to carry things up and down." She looks at her desk, at the wire trays – one black, one white, then at me. "There is another option, of course."

Someone stomps over my grave. Makes me shiver.

"There are some very good homes in the area."

If I had the strength, I'd give her a right dressing down, slam the bloody door on my way out. "What about Grandad? He was here before me. You haven't booted him out."

"We're looking for something suitable for Albert, too. But he is mobile, Jack, so that does make it easier."

"I'd be mobile if you gave me half a chance."

"Just thinking of your wife," Alice says.

How can I object if she puts it like that? "I don't want to be a burden."

"We know that, Dad." Paul takes hold of my hand. Good lad.

Stella dabs at her eyes. Mine are watering, too.

"Why don't you think about it and let me know?" Alice says. She puts the top on her pen and closes the folder.

# Valerie

I head down the corridor that leads to the canteen: just next to Out-patients, opposite Oncology. I need another dose of caffeine to stay awake. I couldn't fly last night. Parents' Evening. The Mums and Dads looked as pissed off as I was. Breakfast was two cappuccinos at the airport, a vodka and tonic and a packet of Swissair nuts on the plane. The flight attendant gave me a funny look. I expect she's more used to serving croissants on the seven-thirty to Heathrow.

"I'll have a large cappuccino, please," I say to the blue-rinsed Women's Institute lady who cocks her head in my direction.

"We don't do cappuccino, I'm afraid," she says. "Haven't got a coffee machine. I can do you a Nescafe, or tea."

"Earl Grey?"

"Tetley's."

"I'll have coffee, please."

"Anything else?"

"No, thanks."

"We do very nice tea cakes?"

"No, just the coffee." I take it to the farthest table, sit looking at the pallid grey brew, feeling as if I've sold my own father.

"Of course he'll have to go," I said, when Mum phoned. She'd never manage him on her own, knock herself out if she tried. She might have forgotten what he was like the first time. I haven't. He had her spinning round the place like a top.

"But it's his house, too. I can't kick him out just because he's getting a bit frail."

"He'll need twenty-four-hour care," I said. Someone's got to be realistic.

"I'll get help from the council. The social worker said a nurse'll come in twice a day."

"What are you going to do the rest of the time? He's got a catheter. Do you want to change his pee bag?"

"If I have to. I've had one myself. It's not the worst thing in the world."

"And what if he falls out of bed in the night? What if he pulls the catheter out?" My voice was an irritable whine, not the BBC calm I was aiming for. "What if he can't control his bowels? Oh, Mum, think about it."

"It's easy for you. You didn't see his face." There was a static-filled pause. "I'm sorry," she sighed. "I just don't know what to do for the best."

I put down the phone and dialled the travel agent's. It was the only rotten thing I could think of.

I'm watching a steady stream of patients in various states of health and hope wander past when someone taps my shoulder.

I look up at Jasmine. Daddy's Girl.

"Mind if I join you?"

There's not much I can do about it. "No."

She puts a Danish pastry and a can of Coke on the table, stifles one yawn, gives in to the next. "Sorry. Just come off my shift."

"I know how you feel," I say, yawning, too.

"Going to see your Dad?"

"I needed some coffee. Don't want to fall asleep at his bedside."

"It must be hard," she says through a mouthful of Danish pastry, "all that travelling."

"Yeah, well. He is my Dad." I sip my coffee, grimace and push it to the centre of the table.

She takes another bite and the apricot filling plops onto the shortie overall she wears instead of a uniform. She wraps it in a tissue and smears the stain into her blue nylon chest. "Messy bugger," she says, shaking her head. "Can't even eat right when I'm knackered."

I nod in complicity. "You'll feel better when you've had a decent sleep."

"I've got work to do on my project. The deadline's next week."

I watch her stuff the remains of the pastry into her mouth. I reach for my coffee, try another sip, give up for good. "That's tough, doing a full day's work then going home to more."

She snaps the ring-pull off the Coke and shrugs. "I need GCSEs for nursing college." She smiles. "Been very helpful to me, your Dad." Slumped over the table, she looks as drained as I feel: bagged, shadowy eyes, spotty, dull skin. "You went to uni, didn't you?"

"Yeah."

"He's always talking about it. How you've done so well for yourself. The other day he said he'd made a lot of mistakes but when he looked at you and your brother, he felt he must have done something right."

I get up from my chair, sniffing and snotty-nosed. "Can I get you another Coke? I fancy one myself."

"No," she says. "I'm fine, but thanks anyway."

On the way out I buy the biggest, shiniest, raisin-stuffed pastry on the counter.

"That's the ticket," the WI lady smiles, "That'll put a bit of flesh on your bones."

*

"Bald," Dad says. In case anyone on this ward and the next hasn't heard, he raises his voice and points at Arthur. "That little man over there."

We clear our throats and fidget. Arthur's wife's back stiffens.

"He is, though," Dad says. "You've got to admit it."

"How are you feeling today?" Mum asks. "We've brought you some fruit cake. Made it myself."

Dad gives her and the cake a dismissive glance. "Stick it up your arse."

"Just you watch it," Jasmine grins as she walks past. "You'll get a right telling off in a minute."

I take Dad's hand. "Why not save it for later? Have it with your cup of tea?"

"Sod fruit cake," Dad says. "I've always bloody loathed it."

I'm not going to contradict him, remind him of the fuss he made on the few Sundays Mum didn't bake one.

"Never mind," she says. "Perhaps you'll fancy a bit tomorrow."

He looks puzzled, blinks, shakes his head. "Are you talking to me?"

Mum nods and takes a hankie out of her bag.

He scowls. "Been talking crap again, have I?"

I squeeze his hand. "No. You just drifted off for a minute."


## Jack

It's always night round here. Days pass so fast. I have a bite to eat, chat with Jasmine, get the occasional visitor then it's night again. I hate the dark, though it does ease my poor head. I keep getting these terrible headaches. Jasmine gives me a couple of Panadol but they do no good. They're not ordinary headaches at the front or back. More like someone's sawn the top off my skull, opened it up to the air. It hurts so much I can hardly see. Blurred shapes, nothing clear. Awful taste in my mouth, like burnt toast.

Bloody hell. Here we go again.

Need to ring for Jasmine. Arm won't work. No feeling.

Christ Almighty! Bayonet slicing through head.

Falling

falling

falling

# Chapter Nine

## May 1996

### Valerie

Dr Duncan stands at the end of Dad's bed, auburn quiff flopping over a face too wrinkled for his years. "He got pneumonia after that last stroke, I'm afraid. We're giving him antibiotics but we don't hold out much hope. I'm sorry."

He's been laid on his side, bones jutting painfully under the sparse bedclothes. I pull the blanket up to his neck. "He doesn't like to be cold."

Duncan folds his stethoscope, stows it in his pocket. "I don't think he'll notice," he says gently.

Mum strokes his face. I rub his shoulder. She yawns, straightens up, flexes her shoulders. "I'll go and phone Paul."

The skin on Dad's wrist is rice paper, eye sockets deep pits, the eyes open but blank. I squeeze his hand, feel a faint answering pressure.

"Just a reflex," Duncan says apologetically. "He's too poorly for a CT scan so we don't know what damage has been done."

I dismiss his words with a flick of my head. Dad knows I'm there.

"Paul's on his way," Mum says.

I get up from the bed. "Just going for a walk round."

On the way off the ward I bump into Lily carrying a brace of empty bedpans. "We don't know how long we can carry on giving him those antibiotics. They're very expensive."

I walk away before I give in to the urge to smash the pans over her slick black head. As I round the corner, I see Paul strolling towards me, a slim, blond suburban Buddha. He wraps me in his arms and I burst into tears. He rubs my back, like Dad used to.

"We must let him go. You know that, don't you?"

Mum points to a small brown phial with bright yellow label. "What's that you're putting in his water?"

Paul hands her the bottle. "Bach Flower Remedies. Nothing that'll harm him."

Mum squints at the label, gives me the bottle.

I put down the vase of bowed-head chrysanths I'm about to chuck. Concentrated Flower Extract, I read. "What's it for?"

Paul takes a second bottle from his jeans pocket. "Giving him two lots. Rescue Drops to help his soul and Walnut to help him let go."

Paul cradles Dad's head, lifts the water to his lips. "Have a little drink, Dad?"

Mum leans across the bed, snatches the glass from Paul's hand and marches off to the sink.

"What did you do that for?" Paul says.

"I'm not having you kill off your Dad."

"This isn't conventional medicine, Mum. It won't have any effect if it's not the right time. If it is, it'll help him."

"Help him die, you mean."

Paul frowns. "Do you want him to live like this?"

"No, of course not." She starts to cry. "I want him to come home."

That's so far beyond reality there's nothing we can say. Paul and I put an arm round her. Our hands meet in the middle of her back.

I pick up the chrysanths. "Let me get rid of these. Then we'll go home. You need a rest. Maybe he'll be brighter tonight."

*

The ward is a solid block of light. Everybody's restless except Dad. Paul and I went out for a quick pizza. Got Mum a sandwich from the canteen. She wouldn't leave him.

"Nurse," Arthur calls. "Help me get up."

"It's not the nurse, Arthur," Paul says. "Not time to get up anyway. You just stay where you are."

"Michael Caine, Michael Caine," Charlie shouts. "I'm over here, Michael. Come and talk to me!"

There's a scurrying under the heap of blankets on Ethel's bed. Then her tiny, wool-swept head pokes out like a baby sparrow waiting to be fed. "I'm going home," she says. "Get me ready. Right now."

"Michael, Michael," Charlie yells. "Michael Caine."

I'm impressed. Looking at Charlie's stained cardi and winceyette pyjamas you'd never guess he moved in celebrity circles.

"I'm sure it's time for me to get up," Arthur says. "They might take me away if I don't."

"Who's making all this racket?" Grandad shouts.

"Michael Caine!"

Rinaldo shakes his head and smiles. "What would Michael Caine be doing in a place like this?"

"If it's those relatives of mine," Grandad says, "you can tell them I'm not going yet."

"Right, Grandad," Rinaldo replies.

Mum pokes her head from behind the screen. "Can't you keep quiet? My husband's very ill."

The large Italian turns as red as the Bolognese sauce he'd love to be eating. "Sorry."

"Michael Caine," Charlie whispers. "Michael Caine. Cheese and onion."

"How is your hubby?" Rinaldo asks.

Mum shakes her head. "No change."

Paul puts his arms round her, rubs her back and shoulders. "You're coming home now. No arguments."

*

Jasmine emerges from behind the screen round Dad's bed. She's been 'cleaning him up,' as she puts it. It's a process we're never allowed to watch, entailing sheets and an octopus collection of tubes. When it's over and we're allowed back, the pupils of Dad's eyes are pointed nails.

"He didn't feel that, did he?" I ask.

"No," Jasmine soothes. "Not a thing."

*

The WI ladies start pouring tea when we walk in, their only question will Mum have chocolate cake today or coffee and walnut? Both home-made. They're very proud of that.

In the corner Fred looks up from the Daily Express. We got chatting last week. He's here every day like us. His wife has cancer of the colon. Terminal. He smiles. "Having a bad day, is he?"

"Another stroke. Now he's got pneumonia."

"Oh, dear. I am sorry."

"How's your wife?"

"Very brave," he nods. "Fighting it every step of the way."

I give Mum a hug, let her cry. In these past few weeks I've touched the pair of them more than in forty-five years.

"What will you have today?"

She pulls away and blows her nose. "Chocolate sponge, I think."

I get tea for two, a mammoth wedge of cake and a Waggon Wheel for myself. Haven't had one of them since the sixth-form tuck shop.

Mum blows on her tea. "It's awful to see him like this. His eyes look so angry."

I fiddle with the wrapper of my Waggon Wheel. "Not angry with you, though."

She bites into the cake, wipes crumbs from her chin. "We had some terrible rows. Perhaps he's remembering them."

"That's all over now, Mum."

She cleans her mouth with a paper serviette. "But his breathing. That dreadful gasping. Do you think he's in pain?"

"The doc says he isn't."

She gazes into her tea cup. "If he were an animal, they'd have put him down weeks ago."

We get up and walk back to the ward, arms round each other's waists.

Mum sits on Dad's bed, smooths the blankets, strokes his hair. "Have you got those drops with you?"

Paul nods.

"Give them to him, then."

*

I'm upstairs in what was my, then Dad's, now is Mum's room, sorting out the white MFI cupboard. It'll keep me occupied for a while. Dad's obsessively tidy, Mum's a magpie with a soft spot for cosmetics. The dregs and final squirts of every face powder, eye shadow, perfume and blusher she's ever bought line the top shelf.

"Can I chuck the really old stuff?" I asked.

"Yes," she said. "Get rid of it all."

The bottom shelf is Dad's. At the back something's sticking out from under a pile of handkerchieves.

*Wir Lernen Deutsch.* German for beginners.

There's an exercise book, too, pages curled with use. The handwriting is Dad's. Big and bold, letters not joined, as if every single one is important. The pages are filled with neatly conjugated verbs. *Leben, lieben, lassen.* Live, love, leave. On the last page he's written one sentence:

*Ich liebe das Leben.* I love life.

I reach into my pocket for a tissue, blow my nose as loud and wet as he did. "I never knew. You were learning bloody German and I never knew."

*

The phone rings at five to twelve. We're squashed on the sofa, Mum and Paul eating brownies and watching Morecambe and Wise, me and Johnnie Walker deep in one of Dad's Wilbur Smiths.

"You stay put, my darlings," Mum says. "Let the old 'un go."

She rushes back into the living room. "Jasmine says the sacral area at the bottom of his back's gone blue. Can we go right away?"

*

August weather in May, brilliant sunshine. Dad's weather. I run upstairs to see if I can get a glimpse of the cars, careful not to trip over Mum's case. She's off to Italy tomorrow. I offered to take her but she said no, she'd rather go on her own. On the other side of the narrow suburban street a maroon Cortina screeches to a halt. A long-lost cousin, the kind that only surfaces at weddings and funerals, gets out. He's wearing a shiny, very tight suit and Ray Bans. Looks like an extra from the *Blues Brothers*.

"Dad's here," I shout, as two Rollers pull up outside the house.

Christ, Dad, I wish you could see this. The second time you've travelled in a limo – my wedding, now your funeral. I run downstairs, grab my handbag.

"Mind where you tread," Paul warns as I step onto the grass verge. "The dustmen have tipped crap all over the place."

I look up, see the coffin in the hearse and howl. Only now does it really sink in. I know you're dead, I was there. But something inside me kept expecting you to come home. Now I realise you won't. You haven't gone to the library or popped round the Paki's to get the papers. This time it's for good. When I stop crying and look at the coffin again, I see it's covered in chrysanthemums; amber, gold, russet, sienna. Rich deep colours.

"Why chrysanths? They his favourites?"

"No," Mum says. "Something private. He'll understand."

The cortege pulls away from the kerb. I wonder why they drive so slowly. I know they can't do a Damon Hill even if it'd amuse you, Dad. Then I realise. The vicar's walking in front of the hearse.

"Is he going to do that all the way?"

"No, dear," Mum smiles. "Just to the end of the road. It's what they always do."

"We'd better go up Turkey Street," the driver says. "Don't want to hold up the traffic on the A10."

We pass the Co-op that's about to close, the bingo hall that used to be a cinema, the long queue that spills out of the Job Centre, turn up Turkey Street then swing onto dual carriageway. At the end of a rose-lined drive we pull up in front of two identical red brick chapels. Getting out of the car, I start to cry again. Paul elbows me softly in the ribs.

"Look at the vicar," he whispers. "His feet."

I glance, blink, look again. Every swish of the cassock reveals, quite plainly for all to see, a pair of silver boots. David Bowie's gone C of E.

"I didn't have the good fortune to know Jack," the pop parson says.

Neither did I, I think, stifling something between a sob and a chuckle. Not for a very long time. That doesn't matter now, though. Now I can admit I am and always have been Daddy's girl.